Content Warning

This fictional work contains the following:

- Explicit sexual content depicted on the page
- Prior emotional abuse and manipulation of a romantic partner
- Prior death of a parent/grandparent
- Profanity
- Stalking

If you are in an abusive relationship, know that it is not your fault. You are worthy of happiness and help is out there. Visit stoprelationshipabuse.org to learn more or call 800-799-SAFE (7233).

First edition April 2024

Cover design created by using licensed materials on Canva

Editing by Emily Michel, www.emilymichel.com

ISBN: 979-8-8689-1336-5

Published by Holly and Oak Publishing

www.islagreggbooks.com

ONE NIGHT *of Fate*

Boston Bears Hockey
Book 1

ISLA GREGG

To all the girls who ever found themselves in a relationship with someone who wanted them to look or act a certain way, this is for you.

Special shout out to the BookTok community. I wouldn't be here if it weren't for your support and encouragement.

ONE NIGHT *of Fate*

Boston Bears Hockey
Book 1

1

Astrid

"My boobs are already sweating," I say to Bailey.

We just stepped out of the airport in beautiful, sunny, hot as absolute fuck Las Vegas. I would have much rather gone to somewhere that has snow to escape the heat of a Boston summer, but Bailey insisted on dragging me to Satan's Butthole.

"Relax, it's only 103 degrees out right now. Besides, it's a dry heat. Your boobs will be dry before you know it," she replies.

It's a damn good thing this is the desert and not some tropical island, otherwise my hair would be getting frizzier by the second.

We make our way over to the rideshare pick up area, where our Uber should be waiting but is nowhere in sight. I check the app and the little car on the map shows it should be right here. *Ugh. I'm melting.*

"Do you see a silver Nissan Sentra?" I ask, trying my best to look around the crowd toward the other end of the pickup area.

"What the fuck is a Nissan Sentra?" Bailey stands on her tiptoes and tries to see around the crowd too. I'm taller than the average woman, but Bailey is barely over five feet tall. There's no way she's seeing anything but the backs of people's heads. More likely, all she's seeing is their shoulders and sweaty armpits.

A silver sedan finally pulls up to the curb, and the driver leans toward the open passenger side window.

"You Astrid?" he calls to Bailey as he throws the car into park.

"No, but she is." She points at me.

The driver hops out and tells us to get in while he loads our suitcases into the trunk. He's a short, tanned, dark-haired man, who looks like he just got in from the Jersey shore.

"So, what brings you ladies to town?" he asks as he pulls away from the curb.

I give Bailey a look that says, "Don't you dare share the embarrassing personal details of my recent breakup with a stranger." She ignores the look.

"Well, it's funny you should ask." She places her hand on my shoulder. "Astrid here was originally supposed to be getting married this weekend."

I groan and curl into myself, as if I can shrivel up and escape the embarrassment of the story Bailey is about to tell. Maybe the driver won't be interested.

"Oh, yeah?" His eyebrows shoot to his receding hairline. "What happened?"

Bailey goes on to tell this man my entire life story. I swear she is the Queen of the Extroverts. She tells him all about how my life fell apart. Listening to her regale our Uber driver with the tale of how my ex-fiancé cheated on me and the subsequent fallout from the end of our relationship does nothing to improve my already salty mood. Thank God Bailey chose a hotel close to the airport for our girls' trip. The short ride means I only have to endure this for the next fifteen minutes.

I block out the conversation happening around me and look out the window as I take in the scenery. I will admit, Las Vegas is beautiful. For being a desert, there are a surprising number of palm trees. As we pull into the main entrance of Mandalay Bay, I feel the stress of the last three months begin to slip away.

Bailey and I climb out of the back seat as her newest friend unloads our luggage. She hooks her arm in mine and says, "Admit it, you're having fun, aren't you?"

I suppress my smile as we turn to head into the lobby. She knows I'm enjoying this, but I'm not about to admit it. Bailey's ego is big enough without me feeding into it.

"Hi there, checking in." She gives her information to the front desk agent while I stand back and admire the lobby.

The pure opulence of the hotel is stunning. My eyes wander from the marble floor to the stately colonnade and up to the chandeliers. As I'm slowly turning around, taking everything in, my eyes land on a group of guys surrounded by a small crowd. They pose for pictures with thumbs up and sign autographs. I don't recognize them as celebrities, but the more I look at them, the more I realize how attractive they are. And they are absolutely *built*.

The one at the center flashes a smile, and through the dark scruff on his chiseled jawline I can see the hint of a pair of dimples. He runs a hand through his dark hair and his black tee shirt stretches so tight across his chest that he might as well be shirtless. The thought of him shirtless sends a thrill through me and straight to my core. Maybe we'll bump into him at the pool? Not that I'd ever have the balls to speak to him. I bet he smells good, too. Hell, I can practically smell his pheromones from here, the man is dripping sex appeal. His ice-blue eyes lock on mine and the breath gets sucked out of my lungs.

"Oh, you are so busted."

Bailey's voice startles me out of the spell, and I nearly jump out of my skin.

"Jesus Christ, you need to get laid. Want me to go introduce you?"

"What? No!" I say way too quickly, glancing back at the hottie with a body. He smirks, clearly amused by my jumpiness. I try to save myself further embarrassment by changing the subject. "Are we all checked in?"

She doesn't push me further to approach Hottie, thank God for small miracles. I can still feel his heated gaze on me as we approach the open elevators. It's another miracle that I wasn't forced to stand there awkwardly waiting for the elevator while his gaze sears into my back. When the doors finally close, I let out the breath I didn't realize I was holding.

"You've got some drool right there." Bailey gestures to the corner of her mouth.

I give her a playful smack on the arm, and we exit the elevator and head to our suite.

***

Several hours of lying by the pool, drinking cocktails, and a spa date later, I feel rejuvenated. Bailey was totally right about this trip. I needed it, mind, body, and soul.

We ate lunch at a weird time while we were at the pool. Now, it's after ten o'clock and even though there are several restaurants we could eat at without leaving the resort, we decide to order takeout. Partly because we're exhausted and just want to put on pajamas, and partly because we want to eat our weight in various desserts where the only witnesses are ourselves and the poor housekeeper who has to remove all the Styrofoam containers tomorrow.

"Oh my God," Bailey says as she scrolls through Door Dash. "Will you judge me if I order food from like three different places?"

I snicker, "Only if you don't judge me for only ordering dessert."

We place our orders, and I hop off my bed to get a shower. I need to wash the pool water out of my hair and the massage oil off my back and legs. The hot water rinses away the last bit of stress I've been holding onto. In the last three months, I've gone from happily engaged to strong, independent woman. There were several very unattractive stops along that route, none of them worth revisiting.

As Bailey gets ready to take her turn in the shower, I throw on a loose-fitted cropped top and a pair of high-waisted leggings. I sit on my bed and start flipping through the guide on the television, looking for a good romantic comedy for Bailey and me to watch while we stuff our faces.

Bailey's voice drifts out of the bathroom. "I just saw a notification pop up from Door Dash. Can you check my phone for me?"

I go into the bathroom and pick up her phone. "Oh shit, the dasher is approaching. I'll run down and grab it."

"You're the best!" she calls as I throw on a pair of sandals and rush out the door.

When I round the corner of the lobby, I realize we may have gone overboard. The annoyed dasher is standing at the concierge desk with an embarrassing amount of food, very obviously from several different restaurants. I shove my room key into the tiny side pocket of my leggings as I approach her, thanking her profusely for bringing all this in. She's not at all grateful for my thanks and leaves as soon as she confirms it's my order, without so much as a goodbye.

The concierge offers to help me, but I wave him off. I've already got half the bags loaded in my arms and I've faced enough embarrassment in this lobby for one day. He wishes me a good night as he loads me up with the last bag, partially blocking my line of sight. I realize as I walk away that there is no way I can shift the bags to press the elevator call button or scan my room key to select the right floor.

Hopefully, there will be someone already there waiting for the elevator who can hit the button for me.

From behind the stack of food containers, I can see the elevator doors start to close.

"Hold the elevator!" I call out as I rush to get there before the door closes. Luckily, whoever is already on the elevator is kind enough to take some pity on me and the doors pop back open.

"What floor?" a smooth male voice asks. I can't see him around this bag, but I do see a big forearm in a navy-blue suit jacket reach out toward the button panel.

"Oh, twenty-nine, please." I reply. When the button doesn't light up, I do my best to gesture toward my left hip. "My key is in my pocket."

I expect him to take some of the bags out of my arms, so I can reach into my pocket, but instead, I feel a warm hand slide between the layers of fabric of my leggings, into the pocket in question. I don't know if I'm breathless from carrying all this food or from his touch. The hand reaches back to the button panel. This time the button stays lit, and the elevator starts its ascent.

I should be extremely creeped out right now. A total stranger just reached down my pants, uninvited. I *should* be running for the hills. But I'm *not* creeped out. I'm so incredibly turned on right now. What is the matter with me? Bailey was right, I *do* need to get laid.

"Here, let me help you," he says as the bag blocking my view is lifted, and I'm suddenly two feet away from the dimpled hottie with a body from this afternoon.

"Oh my God!" I am genuinely shocked to see him, and I instinctively take half a step back and bump into the elevator wall.

"Hi." He smirks.

I try to swallow over the gravel in my throat and collect myself, but all I can do is stare at him. How is it possible for someone to be this attractive? His features up close are just...gorgeous. Can guys be gorgeous? I've been staring at him without saying anything and it's getting weird. I need to break the silence.

"All this food isn't for me." Smooth, Astrid. Real smooth.

He cocks a perfect eyebrow. "Oh?"

Clearly, he's done handing out good deeds and is not going to help me with the conversation. Time to come up with something else.

"I was supposed to get married this weekend," I blurt out. Why the *fuck* would I say that? I glance up to see what floor we're at, we have to be almost there. Oh dear God, we're only at the twelfth floor.

"Oh, so this is for you and your supposed-to-be husband, then?" he says with a smirk. It's clear he's enjoying my awkwardness.

"No, um, it's for me and my friend. He cheated on me." Apparently, it's the day for sharing life stories with strangers.

"Your friend cheated on you?" He's fighting back laughter now. The jerk.

I close my eyes and take a deep breath. "No. My ex-fiancé, Landon, cheated on me three months ago. We were supposed to get married this weekend. The food is for me and my friend, Bailey. She dragged me here to distract me from reality for the weekend."

He shrugs. "Landon sounds like an idiot, if you ask me. I'm Cameron, by the way. You can call me Cam." Giving a half smile, he holds out his hand.

I take his hand and electricity shoots up my arm. "Astrid. Nice to meet you." I try to smile back, but it's hard to do since I no longer have a functioning brain.

When he finally releases my hand, the warmth from his touch lingers on my skin. He keeps his gaze on me as I glance back up to check what floor we're at. Up to twenty now. This must be the slowest elevator in Las Vegas.

"So, you're not from around here then?" he asks.

"What?" I say as my gaze drops from his eyes to his mouth.

"You said your friend dragged you here. I'm assuming that means you're not local?" His tongue flicks out to wet his bottom lip, and my eyes track the slow path his tongue takes across his full lip.

"Oh. Yeah, we flew in this morning." His lips look so soft. I wonder if his kissing is as commanding as his demeanor.

"And since you're not getting married, does that mean you're single?"

Butterflies take flight in my stomach, and I suck in a breath, trying to drive them away. I chew my bottom lip, feeling like I'm in a trance. I don't normally *want* to kiss strangers in elevators. Even if they can wear the *hell* out of a suit. *Ding.* The elevator doors slide open, and I rush into the hall. I don't slow down until I hear the elevator doors close again. I heave a sigh of relief, knowing I'm out from under his spell.

"Astrid." His voice behind me makes me freeze in my tracks.

Even the way he says my name is sexy. I turn around and realize in my rush off the elevator, I left him with one of my food bags and my room key, which he holds up between his index and middle fingers.

"Baby, this won't do me any good if I don't know which room you're in." He saunters toward me, closing the distance as the butterflies return to my stomach.

"Two-oh-one," I say before I realize his implication. "Oh! That's not what I—"

"Relax, I'm just messing with you." He smirks, allowing me a glimpse of his dimples through the scruff on his jaw. "Let me help you to your room. There's no way you're going to be able to open the door without losing at least one of these bags."

I scold myself. He's clearly not affected at all by our interaction. I'm just reading too much into things. "That's okay but I—"

"Okay, let's see," he says, looking at the sign indicating the direction of my room, "201 is this way." He turns in the opposite direction of the one I was headed. That's embarrassing.

Sighing, I follow him down the hall toward my room. Since he can't see me, I shamelessly check out his build. It's impressive. He must be six foot five, at least. His broad shoulders taper down slightly to his hips. I don't know if I've ever checked out a man's ass before, but this guy has the ass of a god. I continue my downward sweep over his body, down his thick thighs that I can only imagine are as toned and hard as the rest of his body. The thought of digging my nails into his hard muscles sends a shiver down my spine. He has enough sex appeal to talk the panties off anyone.

And now I'm thinking about him taking off my panties. Bailey was definitely right. I need to get laid.

When he reaches my room, he sets down the bags he was carrying and turns toward me. "It was nice to meet you, Astrid."

I set down my own bags and my eyes rest on his lips again. "It was nice to kiss you, too." Wait, what did I just say?

He chuckles, flashing one dimple and wetting his bottom lip again. I hope Bailey didn't hear that, she will never let me hear the end of it if she did.

He places his warm hands on my hips and tugs me closer. He brings his mouth closer to me until I'm sure he can feel my heavy breathing hitting his face. When I finally tear my eyes away from his mouth and meet his heated gaze, he takes the opportunity. He presses his lips to mine in a soft embrace. The kiss is gentle and chaste, but its effect on me is anything but. Energy rips through me, and the earth quakes underneath me. He pulls back and I meet his gaze again.

Swallowing hard, I let out a shaky breath. "Cameron—"

The protest dies on my lips as his mouth comes crashing back into mine. His hands tighten like a vise on my hips. I reach up and tangle my fingers through his hair, pulling him tighter against my face. He parts his lips, and our tongues meet. He pulls my hips into him, using the pressure to turn us and press me against the door. Once I'm against a solid surface, he grinds his hips into me, and it's obvious he's enjoying this as much as I am. I arch my back and push my breasts up into his chest. He responds with a growl and pulls his mouth from mine to trail hot kisses down my neck.

"You like that, don't you, baby?" His raspy voice is barely above a whisper in my ear. I instinctively angle my hips, looking for some friction. He lets out a low chuckle and brings his thigh between my legs. "Don't worry, I'll give you what you want."

I grind my hips against him as he reaches under my shirt and cups my breasts. I need his mouth on mine again. He's an amazing kisser. Like seriously awesome, but I think he's enjoying watching me squirm a little too much. I let out a gasp when he reaches lower with his free hand and kneads my ass, pressing me harder against his growing erection.

"If I put my hand down your pants, are you going to be wet for me?" He has the dirtiest mouth. I wonder if he always talks this dirty. I think I like it.

I answer with a moan, and he silences me with his mouth. He moves his thigh between my legs, giving me the perfect amount of pressure and friction through my leggings to ease some of the ache. Oh God, I might come if he keeps this up.

It is at this exact moment that I feel the door give way behind me, knocking me off balance. Cameron stops us from falling into the suite—another display of his obvious strength. He must be some kind of weightlifter or something.

Being blocked by Cameron in front of me and Bailey behind me, I take my only escape route by stepping to the side. The problem with that plan, though, is that I forgot I have a set of take-out bags on either side of me. My foot catches and I nearly fall again as my feet fail to gain any purchase. Once again, Cameron keeps me upright. His reflexes are incredible and once I untangle my feet and finally stand on my own, my eyes bounce between an amused Cameron and a bewildered Bailey.

"No need to stop on my account. I'm just going to grab these," Bailey says as she motions toward the bags.

"You must be Bailey." Cameron's smooth voice and warm smile ooze sex appeal as he stretches his hand out to greet her. "I'm Cameron."

Bailey smiles and shakes his hand. "Nice to meet you." She levels me with a stern look, then winks as she grabs the takeout bags. "Don't do anything I wouldn't do."

Yeah, right. Bailey is the queen of random hookups. I'm pretty sure there isn't much she wouldn't do when it comes to sex.

The door closes behind her with a click. There's a beat of awkward silence as I realize my breathing is still heavy.

"I should go," I say as I reach for the door handle. When it doesn't immediately give way, I remember that Cameron still has my key.

He smiles and holds the key up in the air. "You'll probably need this."

I snatch it out of his grasp, and I glare at his back as he turns to leave.

"So, I have to ask." He spins around, surprising me. "I saw you staring at me in the lobby today. I thought you recognized me, but after that elevator ride, I'm not convinced." He scrubs his hand over his scruff and looks humble for the first time since I saw him in the lobby.

I'm a little taken aback for a moment before I recover. "Was that a line? Does that actually work on women?" I fight back a giggle.

He looks offended, and a little hurt. "No, usually women know who I am before they stick their tongue down my throat."

I bristle at this cocky bastard. "First of all, you introduced yourself to *me.* Secondly, I did *not* stick my tongue down your throat." I take a step closer to him in challenge.

He smirks. "Baby, your teeth were behind my teeth."

I gape at him, opening my mouth to say something, but I'm at a total loss for words. I turn and hold the key to the sensor. "And to answer your question, no. I have no idea who you are, and I'd kind of like to keep it that way, to be honest."

He takes a few steps backwards, laughing. "It was nice to kiss you too, Astrid."

He walks away as I push my way into my room.

2

Cameron

I've been tossing and turning all night. Each time I drift off, I see Astrid. What a woman. When I saw her in the lobby before the game tonight, I almost walked up and introduced myself. I was kicking myself all night for missing the opportunity. She just about jumped out of her skin when her friend caught her giving me an eye-fuck. I'll be honest, I was eye-fucking her right back. She was beautiful, but not in a way that was forced, with revealing clothing or heavy makeup. Her natural beauty shone like a beacon across the lobby, drawing me in. I couldn't stop thinking about her all night. It might have played a small part in our loss tonight.

As a professional athlete, I need to be laser focused. Especially in the playoffs. During the Stanley Cup finals? I have no room for any kind of distraction. An NHL player's career only lasts so long, and you never know which game is going to be your last. I've been a center for the Boston Bears for eight seasons now, the last three of which I've served as captain. And our loss tonight against Las Vegas? They got lucky.

We won the first two games of the finals at home. The whole team was hoping we would make a clean sweep and win games three and four on the road this weekend. But in typical Vegas fashion, the house won.

Hockey players are a superstitious bunch. Case in point, the playoff beard. Every team in the league has their own good luck rituals, and ours is no different. For away games, we go to whatever bar or restaurant is on site at whatever hotel we're staying at, and we open a single tab. The whole team has at least one round, usually paid for by one of the more tenured players. Sometimes a rookie will feel generous with his new contract burning a hole in his pocket, and offer to pay the tab. Until he realizes how quickly twelve bucks per beer for twenty-three players adds up, and most guys stay for three rounds, if not more. I offered to pay tonight, mostly because I knew I was only going to stay for the first round.

The guys gave me so much shit for calling it an early night, but I gave them my disapproving captain's look and told them I'd tell Coach they were at a strip club all night. The threat of Coach's wrath was enough to shut them up. They knew they'd be doing speed drills first thing at tomorrow's morning skate otherwise. Besides, they were happy to continue to drink on my tab whether I was there or not.

As it turns out, I'm lucky I left when I did. If I hadn't, I wouldn't have run into Astrid. She was so fucking adorable trying to carry enough food to feed our starting lineup. When I took the bag that was hiding her face from my view, her beauty floored me again. She looked like she had gotten some sun since I saw her in the lobby. Her dark brown hair was piled up on top of her head in a messy bun, still wet and smelling like shampoo. And again, no makeup, not that she needed any.

I would be lying if I said I didn't want to kiss her. She had awkwardly dropped the fact that she was newly single due to her fiancé's infidelity, and their June wedding was supposed to be this weekend, no less. Talk about the prime time for a woman to make a bad decision and fall into bed with a hot, muscular, NHL-playing stranger. I'm always in favor of a one-night stand, especially if it's while we're on the road. Hometown hookups leave too much room for the promise of a relationship, and that is something I just can't commit to with my schedule.

With as jumpy as she was, I knew there was a fine line between letting her know I wanted her and scaring her away. When she revealed what she was thinking and said "Nice to kiss you" instead of "Nice to meet you," I decided a light kiss on her perfect lips straddled that line quite nicely.

That first kiss was anything but soft and sweet. I swear I could feel the earth crumble from under my feet. The intensity was surprising. When I pulled back and looked into those dark green eyes of hers and heard my name on her lips, I forgot all about the line I was walking and jumped in headfirst.

I can still hear her breathless little moans when I talked dirty in her ear. I wonder what she sounds like when she comes. My level of interest in her was apparent from the tenting going on in the front of my suit pants. I was about to find out her own level of interest before the door swung open and she tripped over the takeout bags like a newborn baby deer standing for the first time.

The interruption was a relief. I wouldn't have been able to stop myself otherwise, and she didn't seem like the type of woman who has one-night stands on a regular basis. I gave her an out by not resuming our kiss as soon as we were alone again, which she took. But damn, I wish she hadn't.

Now, I know I made the right decision by leaving. Some women, especially those fresh out of a committed relationship, feel guilty after a hookup. Sex is supposed to be fun. But that fun would have been ruined for me if she woke up with regrets in the morning. I didn't want it to go down like that.

I glance at the time on my phone. It's after four in the morning, and I only have a little over two hours before I have to be up and on the bus heading to our morning practice. I haven't gotten more than a few hours of sleep, but that's pretty normal for me, especially on the road.

Today is our day off between games, if you can call it that. We spend most of the day at the arena, practicing, reviewing strategy, watching videos of Las Vegas's games from this season. By the time our coach releases us at almost four in the afternoon, I'm beat.

"Hey man." Justin smacks me on the shoulder as we make our way to the team bus. "What was up with you this morning? You seemed distracted."

Justin is my oldest and closest friend. We met in the second grade, when his family moved to our small town in upstate New York. We grew up playing hockey together and I consider him to be my brother, both on and off the ice.

"Just trying to take it easy." I shrug, hoping he buys it.

He doesn't. "You never take it easy, especially in the finals."

I glare at him. "I took a hard hit last night."

"Bullshit. What's on your mind?"

He's known me long enough to know when I'm lying. And I've known him long enough to know that he will continue to ask about it until I tell him. He's one stubborn bastard.

"I met a girl last night—"

"Nice!" He cuts me off and offers a fist bump. "I figured that's why you left the bar early."

I shake my head, and he finally lets his fist fall. "We didn't hook up."

"Why not? You choke?" He elbows me in the side.

I glare at him. Justin always gives me a hard time for wanting to set the mood with a woman before having sex with her. In his mind, sex is the main course. For me, it's more like the last in a two-course meal.

He throws up his hands in surrender. "Listen man, you need to find a way to close the deal before the game tomorrow. You played like shit this morning."

"I was not that bad." I'm actually offended. Sure, I missed a few shots, but I was shooting against our star goalie. The dude can stop anything. There's a reason he's number one in the league.

He levels me with a glare. "Cam. Dude. You looked like a high school junior varsity team's defenseman trying to play center for the first time."

Justin is always blunt and to the point. I usually enjoy his brutal honesty *if* it's aimed at someone else. When it's aimed at me, it's not so fun.

"Look, you obviously need to get laid," he states like it's a fact. If Justin was Larry the Cable Guy, sex would be his duct tape. It's his fix for everything.

"I do not need to get laid."

"You do," he pushes. "We don't need some snot-nosed JV kid. We need our captain. You need to find that girl and close the deal."

I have been thinking about Astrid all day. How soft her lips were. The smell of her shampoo. Her unabashed willingness to grind up against me in the hallway, where anyone could see us, taking what she needed from me. There's nothing that turns me on more than watching a woman come undone from my touch. I'm sure she was teetering on the edge and would have come if her friend hadn't interrupted us.

"You know I'm right, man." He claps me on the back again before climbing onto the bus.

On the ride back to the hotel, all I can think about is Astrid. How desperate her kiss was, what it felt like when she was grinding on my leg. My cock starts to swell at the memory of her whimpering when I cupped her pussy. Justin might be right about me needing to get laid.

As we walk into the lobby, I can't keep myself from scanning the crowd for Astrid. She's not there, which is both a relief and a disappointment. I definitely need a shower and could use a little manscaping before I track her down and convince her to come back to my room.

After my shower, I get in the elevator to stop by her room and see if she's there. It's not until the elevator doors have closed that I realize I can't get to her floor. My key card only works for the floor my own room is on, the lobby, and other public spaces in the hotel. I sigh in resignation, realizing my only option is to go to the lobby and hope I run into her.

I spend the next two hours wandering around the lobby, trying not to look like a creep as I watch every single person getting on or off the elevator.

"Oh man!" An excited voice says, "Are you CJ Grant?"

Suddenly, I'm surrounded by about ten energetic high-school-aged kids with a couple chaperones. They're all wearing the same printed tee shirt, here on a class trip by the looks of it. They all start asking me for autographs, photos, and a million questions. I am so distracted by the teenage chaos that I almost don't see Astrid as she crosses the lobby to the bank of elevators, Bailey at her side and nearly a dozen shopping bags between them.

It plays out the same way as it did yesterday. We lock eyes for a moment as she passes, and the entire world shifts into slow motion. All the voices around me are suddenly muffled. The wind is knocked out of me like I just got checked into the boards. I realize, as she stands to one side to let people off the elevator, that if I don't get away from this group of teenagers right the fuck now, I'm going to miss her. She steps onto the elevator, and I say a hasty goodbye to the group. I run at a full sprint and make it there just in time to stick my hand between the doors and stop the elevator from leaving.

I breathe a sigh of relief as I step onto the elevator. Astrid gawks at me while Bailey takes the chance to greet me.

"Hi Cameron!" she says warmly. "Astrid and I were *just* talking about you."

I raise my eyebrows in surprise and shift my gaze over to Astrid.

Astrid puts her hands up in the air defensively. "We were not—"

Bailey cuts her off. "Astrid was saying how much she *enjoyed* meeting you yesterday and how much she hoped she would run into you again so you guys could exchange numbers." Bailey gives her a nudge toward me.

I can't help but smile at that. So, she was thinking about me as much as I was thinking about her. "I'm glad I caught you then. I was just going to ask Astrid here if she wanted to get a drink with me."

Astrid gets the prettiest little flush across her cheeks.

Bailey answers for her. "She would love to."

"Great," I say, looking at Astrid. "It's a date."

Astrid gives her friend a death glare. "It's not a date and can we please stop talking about me as if I'm not here?"

Bailey lowers her voice and leans into her ear. "We talked about this. What's the harm in having a little fun? This will be good for you."

She speaks back to her through clenched teeth. "We also talked about how I'm not interested in hooking up with random strangers on vacation."

I don't think they realize I can hear them, so I chime in. "It's just a drink," I say. "No pressure for anything more than that."

They exchange a look, and I get the sense that they've been friends for a while.

Finally, Astrid sighs and says, "Fine. One drink. In the lobby bar."

I pretend to mull over her offer and counter. "How about we do three drinks, in my room?"

"Two drinks, lobby bar." The corner of her mouth lifts in a suppressed smile.

"One drink, my room." I cock a brow.

She can't hold back the smile now and her eyes drop to the floor as she shakes her head. She's got a beautiful smile.

"Deal," she exhales.

The elevator dings as it reaches their floor.

"Well, this is my stop. Have fun, you two." Bailey takes the bags from Astrid and bounces off the elevator.

I scan my room key and hit the button for the thirty-third floor. There's a beat of silence and I decide to break it. "You look great, by the way," I say, looking her up and down.

She rolls her eyes. "Shut up." She sounds annoyed, but her smile gives her away as the doors open again.

I chuckle to myself as I walk off the elevator, Astrid keeping close by my side, right where I want her.

I scan the room key and hold the door open ahead of me for Astrid. She walks past me, her arm brushing lightly against my abdomen, making my muscles quake.

"Make yourself at home," I tell her as I let the door close behind me and go to inspect the drink options in the minibar. I frown at the limited selection. "I have beer and a few tiny bottles of super cheap vodka."

Astrid chuckles, "Beer is fine." She kicks off her sneakers and sits cross-legged on the foot of the bed.

I crack open two bottles and pass her one. "Cheers." I hold out my bottle toward her.

"Cheers." She clinks her bottle to mine and we both take a long sip while eyeing each other.

I sit across from her in the armchair. I figure if I put some distance between us, then neither one of us will be tempted to do something we regret. By we, I mean Astrid. I'd let this woman do anything to me at this point. All she needs to do is ask.

The memories from our kiss the day before flood my senses. If there's anything she wants from me, I hope she asks soon. I don't know how long I'll be able to keep my hands off her.

"So, where are you from?" I ask, genuinely curious to get to know her a little better.

She grimaces. Not a good sign. "Cameron," she starts.

I put up a hand. "You can call me Cam. Cameron makes me feel like I'm five and getting in trouble."

She laughs before continuing. "Cam, I'm not interested in getting into another relationship right now. The last one ended horribly, and I just can't do it again." She looks at me regretfully, which is not a look I was hoping to be on the receiving end of tonight.

I give her a nod. "I get it. You don't want to get hurt."

"Exactly." She looks relieved.

I raise the beer bottle to my mouth as she continues.

"I just want to have wild, reckless, no strings attached, hotel room sex with a stranger."

I cough, choking on my beer.

"Shit, are you okay?" Her face is full of concern.

I nod as I continue to cough, finally clearing my throat. "I'm good."

"Anyway," she takes a deep breath. "I was hoping you might be the man for the job." She looks at me and bites her bottom lip.

Blood rushes to my cock. I stand and close the distance between us. After taking her bottle of beer and setting it down on the dresser, I hold my hand out to her. "Come here." My voice is thick with desire.

She takes my hand and stands. I wrap my arms around her waist, and she hooks her hands together behind my neck but keeps her eyes on my mouth.

"I'll be your man for the night." I lift her chin when she still doesn't meet my gaze. "But you have to promise me something."

She raises an eyebrow in question and bites her bottom lip again. My cock throbs at the sight.

"You have to promise me you won't regret having sex with someone you'll never see again."

She swallows. "Done. I have no regrets."

Thank *fuck.* I tighten my arms around her and press my throbbing cock into her abdomen, brushing my lips over hers. "You will when I'm done with you."

Whatever protest she was about to make dies on her lips as I seal my mouth to hers. I part my lips as she does the same, our tongues exploring each other's mouths. She sucks on my lower lip, and I let out a groan.

I pull back to pepper kisses down her neck, looking for the sensitive spot that made her moan my name last night. She draws in a sharp breath and arches her back, grinding against me. I lock my lips back on hers as I feel her gentle tug at the hem of my shirt. We break apart just long enough for me to help her pull it over my head. I tease her, skimming my fingertips around the waistband of her jeans, and she rocks her hips into me again.

Pulling her shirt off, I continue kissing a path down her neck and across her collarbone. Reaching up, I begin kneading one of her perfect breasts over her bra. She tightens her fingers in my hair, trying to push my head lower, but I stay put. She counteracts my stubbornness by reaching behind her back, unclasping her bra, and throwing it to the floor.

She has the most beautiful round tits that fill the palm of my hand. I pinch one nipple and she moans, pressing her mouth to the side of my neck and sucking hard. I'm definitely going to have a hickey tomorrow. Which is fine, she can mark me however she wants.

I let out another groan. She's not going to let me take this slow. She starts messing with my belt, but I grab her wrist to stop her.

"Not yet, baby. You're going to come for me before you get my cock."

I reach down and unfasten the button on her jeans. She shimmies them down her hips and kicks them off before grabbing me and pulling my mouth to hers. Our tongues continue exploring each other's mouths, while my cock throbs, painfully hard behind the zipper of my jeans.

I lean down and hook my hands under her ass, picking her up as she wraps her legs around me. I walk us to the bed and practically throw her onto the mattress. I unfasten my belt and kick off my jeans before joining her on the bed.

Our mouths meet again as I settle between her legs. She rocks her hips up and I can feel how wet she is through the thin fabric of her panties. I kiss down her neck and suction my mouth to one of her nipples.

She lets out a small whimper. I don't know if I've ever been this turned on by the sounds someone makes during sex. Her little moans and whimpers are way sexier than anything I've ever witnessed.

I continue to trail kisses down over her ribs to the arch of her hip bone, my hand mimicking my mouth's path on the other side of her body. I hook my fingers into the waistband of her panties, and she lifts her hips to let me pull them down. Sitting back on my knees, I admire her naked body, splayed out on my bed, just for me.

"So beautiful," I murmur as I twist my arms under her knees and pull her down to me.

She lets out a little squeal followed by a giggle.

"Oh, you like it when I'm rough with you?" I say as I nip at her inner thigh.

She answers with a moan. I take a finger and run it over her slit, through the wetness pooling there. She moans again and rocks her hips, desperate for more. I kiss from her thigh up to the crease of her hip and suck hard. She threads her fingers through my hair and pulls. I bite her other thigh, enjoying teasing her. She's so responsive to every touch. I take a finger and press it into her soaking pussy.

"Cam," she breathes.

I groan again at the sound of my name and circle her clit with my tongue. She gasps and bucks her hips, surprising me. I add a second finger to her soaking wet pussy and feel her muscles tighten around them. I glance up at her and she's propped up on her elbows, watching me and pinching one of her nipples. I love watching women touch themselves, it's one of my biggest turn-ons.

She lets out a loud moan when I suction my mouth to her clit and add a third finger. She's building up to an orgasm in what is probably a new record for me. I suck her clit deep into my mouth, working it with my tongue, pumping my fingers in and out of her tight pussy.

Every muscle in her body suddenly tenses, and I know she's about to come apart.

"That's it, baby. Come for me," I say before sealing my mouth on her clit.

She cries out, hips bucking wildly as her orgasm slams into her. I groan too, unbelievably turned on by the knowledge that I did this to her. And now that sweet pussy is coming all over my fingers and my face.

As she comes down from the high, her fingers tug at my hair, pulling me up to her. She seals her mouth to mine before I have a chance to wipe off some of the extra juices that have stuck to my beard. I didn't think it was possible to get any more turned on than I already am, but a woman willingly, and greedily, tasting her own come does the trick.

I kick off my boxers and settle down next to her as we continue to kiss and make out. My swollen cock throbs against her leg and she reaches down, smiling against my mouth when my cock throbs in her hand.

She pushes me down onto my back and I go willingly, mesmerized by the sight of her trailing kisses down my chest and scratching her fingernails over my abs.

"You're so hot," she says, continuing lower.

"You don't have to do that." A lot of women don't enjoy having a dick in their mouths, especially one as big as mine.

"I want to," she coos, giving me a devilish grin.

I watch her close a hand around the base of my shaft, then stack her other hand on top of it. Nearly half of my cock still sticks out above her hands. She pumps and twists her hands around my shaft, up to the head and back down again.

"Your cock is huge," she says with a big smile on her face.

"You're great for a guy's ego, you know that?" I brush my fingers through her hair, keeping it out of her face as she settles on her knees between my legs.

I watch as she wraps her pretty little lips around the head and sucks. She meets my eyes as she releases it with a light popping sound. She leans further down and gives the underside a lick from the base all the way up to the tip, swirling her tongue around the head.

"So sexy," I whisper to her.

She gives me a little smirk and raises one eyebrow. "Oh yeah?"

"Yea—" My affirmation turns into a moan as she sinks her mouth down onto my cock. She takes me all the way to the back of her throat and swallows, and I swear I see stars. "Oh my God, Astrid."

She hums, sending a shockwave straight into my balls. She inches off my cock at an agonizingly slow pace, pumping with one hand and kneading my balls with the other. I watch as she crouches lower, taking one of my balls into her mouth and sucking gently. I rise onto my elbows to get a better look, thanking God I had the forethought to manscape earlier. Astrid has a hand between her legs.

"Are you fingering yourself?" I've never seen a woman get this turned on by giving a blowjob before. I think I love it.

"Uh-huh," she hums innocently, taking my cock so deep into her throat it negates all the innocence in her tone.

"Oh, no you don't," I rasp, twisting to the side and curling my arm under her hips. "That's my job."

She lets out a little squeal as I swing her hips up on top of me. She settles her knees on either side of my head, and I have the perfect close-up view of her soaking wet pussy.

I flatten my tongue and lick from her clit to her opening, twirling my tongue around the edge and pushing it inside her.

She gasps and then shoves my cock into the back of her throat again.

I groan and rock my hips. Astrid is already taking me so deep, but I ache for more.

She grinds against my face, and I suction my lips to her clit and start pumping my fingers into her pussy again. She matches my rhythm with her mouth on my cock.

I'm trying desperately to get Astrid off again before I lose myself in her mouth. As good as her mouth feels, I want to bury my cock deep inside her when I come. I try to focus on making her come, but the closer she gets, the wilder she gets with my cock. It's like a race to see who can come apart first and we're both sprinting to the finish line.

I feel her legs start to stiffen as her rhythm falters and I know she's close. I reach around her hip and clamp my arm down, holding her tight against me.

She moans, coming apart on my face, writhing from the pleasure. I don't think she realizes she's doing it, but she squeezes my cock so hard that I almost come apart with her. I guide her gently down from her orgasm, impressed with myself that this one was just as intense as the first. This next part is going to be fun.

3

Astrid

Cameron has a magic mouth. I've never had someone who could make me come with their mouth. *Ever*. Landon would spend what seemed like hours down there with minimal pressure, minimal finger action, and I usually lied, telling him I needed his dick before I got anywhere close to coming. He never clamped his mouth down on my clit like Cameron just did. It happened so fast. I've never had an orgasm slam into me like that once, let alone twice. I lost all control and I swear I saw stars.

This is already the best sex I've ever had, and we haven't even technically had sex yet. But we're about to. I climb off his face—another thing I've never done—and kneel on the bed in front of him. Cameron sits up and pulls me toward him, so I'm straddling his legs. His enormous cock rises between us, and I can feel it pulse as we make out. In another first, I've never kissed anyone right after they went down on me. I've never wanted to, but something about Cameron turns me on so fiercely that I would do and try anything with him.

I don't know what it is about Cameron, but I feel different with him than I've ever felt before. Something about him makes me feel so secure in myself that I don't mind asking for what I want, not that I've had to ask for anything yet. He seems to know what I need before I do. He's gotten me off twice with his mouth without me so much as breathing a word of guidance.

I'm shamelessly grinding up against his erection, which is enormous. I'm anxious about if it's going to hurt. He breaks our kiss to suck on my nipple, and I bite my lip to stifle another moan. With as wet as I am, if I just rose up a bit, I could slip his cock right into my pussy.

"I want you inside me," I say softly. I can't wait to find out how he fucks. If it's half as good as his mouth game, it's going to be awesome.

He lets out a soft laugh. "Don't worry, baby. We'll get there," he says before giving my other tit some attention.

Hearing him call me baby, it does something to me. And I like it.

"Cameron, please. I want your cock." I'm not above begging.

He lets out a groan, wraps an arm around me, and flips us over so I'm lying under him. I've never been thrown around during sex, and I'm so unbelievably turned on by it.

Cameron sits back on his knees and has a condom on before I even realize he's gotten one out. I spread my legs wider, and he hovers over me. He rubs the head of his cock over my clit before guiding it lower and inching just the head in.

I suck in a breath and press the back of my head into the pillow. He's so thick, I don't think it's going to fit. I squeeze my eyes shut as he tries to press in deeper.

"Astrid," he says so quietly I'm not sure I've heard him. He pulls back a bit as he readjusts his weight.

I open my eyes and see him looking at me with the softest expression. He reaches up, cupping my cheek, and looks deep into my eyes.

"Try to relax, baby." He kisses me gently.

I try to focus on the kiss while I get used to his size. Cameron doesn't move an inch, but when he trails kisses down my neck and pinches my nipple, I rock my hips without even realizing, and feel myself being stretched as his cock sinks deeper.

"That's it, baby. You're taking me so well."

I let out a loud moan as he sinks another inch lower, and I tense up again.

"Breathe for me," he whispers as he eases his cock out at an agonizingly slow pace.

I relax a little bit before he reverses his direction and starts easing back inside me again. He lets out a loud groan as he finally gets his entire length fully seated.

"Fuck baby, you're tight," he breathes against my ear.

He starts a slow, steady rhythm, easing almost the entire way out before slowly sinking back in. The sensation of his cock stretching me sends a jolt of electricity up my spine.

And every time he reaches the sweet spot deep inside me, I can't see straight.

Pretty soon, the slow pace he's been keeping isn't enough for either of us. He reaches down and grabs one of my legs, lifting it up and changing the angle. I rock my hips up to meet him, and he puts his hand between us, rubbing a thumb over my clit. I can feel the coils of another orgasm tightening in my core.

"Harder," I moan, locking my feet behind him, pulling him even deeper.

He moves his hand from my clit to under my ass, pulling me up slightly so he's grinding against my clit.

"Astrid—" he gasps. "Let go, baby. I'm right there with you."

His words are all it takes. The thin coils holding me together snap and I come apart again. Every thrust sends shock waves through me, and I hear his mumbled curses that signal his own release only a second after my own.

He collapses beside me, looking exhausted and fully satisfied. "That was amazing," he says between heavy breaths.

I roll over to my side, propping myself up on my elbow. "Wanna do it again?"

I'm only half joking. That was some seriously amazing sex and I'm not ashamed to say I want more.

He smiles, leans in, and presses his lips to mine in a quick kiss. "Don't go anywhere, okay?"

I bite my lip and nod in response, watching as he bounces up off the bed and struts across the room and into the bathroom, all the tightly coiled muscles of his back on display.

"Give me like ten minutes, then I'll be good to go." He leans out of the bathroom and wags his eyebrows at me. "Want me to go down on you again?"

I laugh, "I was just kidding. I don't know that I can handle another orgasm."

"You most certainly can, and I wasn't joking. Give me ten minutes and we can go again." He calls over the sound of the sink running.

"There is no way that's possible," I say dryly.

"What's not possible?" His frame fills the doorway into the bathroom. "Whether I'll be able to go again or your ability to handle another orgasm?"

I admire his naked body from across the room. He probably is the most muscular guy I've ever laid eyes on. And he's tall. There's only five or six inches between the door frame and his dark, tousled hair. My gaze travels lower, over his strong chest. The man has abs for day. Maybe weeks. And lower, the deep cut V of his hips points directly to the most impressive part of his anatomy.

The way he's looking at me makes me feel way more naked than I already am. But, for as exposed as I feel, I'm equally at ease. Maybe it's the fact that I know this is a one-time thing. Maybe it's the fact that he's so attractive and I know there's no way he'd ever be with me in real life.

Maybe it's the fact that there are no expectations attached. Something about him just makes me feel safe and secure.

"Well, both actually." I give him a half smile. "I've never had someone give me more than one orgasm." The flush creeps up into my cheeks and I look down, pretending to pick at some stray lint on the sheets.

"There's no way that's possible." He saunters over to the bed and settles in beside me, propped up on one elbow.

"It's true. My ex was..." I mull over how to phrase this. "Let's just say he didn't make me feel wanted."

He cups the back of my neck and brushes his thumb along my cheekbone. "Your ex was an idiot, then." He gives me a light kiss. "In more ways than one."

I give him a weak smile and fidget with the sheets, picking at some more imaginary fuzz.

"Hey," he says, lifting my chin. "Astrid, I'm serious. I don't know you well, but you'd have to be completely oblivious to not realize what an incredibly rare woman you are."

I feel myself flush again. I can tell that he's being sincere. Under normal circumstances, I might let myself catch feelings after a statement like that. I remind myself that, whatever I'm feeling right now, it's only for tonight. Tomorrow, I'll be back in Boston, and he'll be... I have no idea where he'll be. That's the point, right?

"Come here," he says. He rolls onto his back and puts an arm around me, tucking me into his side. "I'm a firm believer in the phrase 'Everything happens for a reason.'

Just think, right now, you could be having the most underwhelming sex with your newlywed husband. Instead, you're here with me, having the most incredible sex you never even thought was possible."

I act offended and give him a playful smack on the chest. "You're so full of yourself."

He levels me with a glare. "Look me in the eye and tell me that wasn't the best sex you've ever had with a complete stranger."

"Oh, I'm not saying it wasn't good." I smile up at him. "But I don't have anything to compare it to, so I can't be sure."

He gives me a devilish smile and rolls back onto his side, pressing on my lower back and pulling me tightly against him. "I could give you something to compare it to right now."

He kisses me deeply and I realize that he's being literal. His cock is already perking back up.

"I suppose." I smile against his lips. "But purely for scientific purposes, not for enjoyment."

He kisses down my neck. "Maybe we should repeat the experiment a few times. Just until a pattern can be identified."

I let out a giggle and jump when his fingers skim my waistline.

He gives me a surprised look. "Are you ticklish?"

"No," I lie.

“Oh,” he says, going back to kissing my neck and skimming his fingers over my curves. “So, if I do this—" He rests his hand directly at my waistline and looks way too excited.

“Cam—” I warn.

He squeezes the soft spot between my ribs and hip bone. I jump and squeal, laughing and trying to wriggle free. Before I even realize it, Cam is on top of me, my wrists trapped in one of his hands and pinned above my head. My chest heaves from the excitement, and I feel his warm breath skimming my bare breasts.

He closes his mouth over one peaked nipple, and I can’t help but let out a loud moan.

“Enough fun,” he kisses his way down my stomach. “Let’s test out my theory.”

4

Cameron

I'm having second thoughts about this being just a one-time fling. The sex is amazing. Astrid is fun to joke with and I feel like I can talk to her about anything. The best part is, she's an incredible woman. I want to ask her for her number, exchange last names, follow her on Instagram, anything that means that I might be able to get in touch with her after this. But she was crystal clear: what happens in Vegas, stays in Vegas.

As a professional athlete, it's incredibly difficult to meet people outside the hockey bubble. I take that back, it's very easy to meet people. It's difficult to meet *genuine* people—people who like me for me. More often than not, I find out too late that someone is showing an interest in getting to know me for the wrong reasons. For some people, it's the money. For others, it's the allure of being in the public eye. And let's not forget about the puck bunnies.

It's not that I have a "zero bunny" policy. I've hooked up with a few. The problem is that, for the few that I have hooked up with, it hasn't ended well. The puck bunnies are notorious for only wanting to get close to hockey players just to be able to say that they got close to a hockey player. Some will do anything to blur the line of a boundary you've set. I found that out the hard way last season. Now I have to coordinate my safety with the local police. I push the thought away. Astrid is different.

Astrid is probably the most genuine person I've ever met. It's obvious that there's more to the story about what went down with her ex, but I get the sense it's not because she's trying to paint herself in a better light. It seems more like she's put it behind her and has moved on with her life. Which is strange, considering this all went down only three months ago.

There's one thing for sure, if I was her man, no way in hell I would find myself in bed with another woman. Astrid is way too much fun to have sex with. She's so responsive to every touch. And she's not shy about taking what she needs during sex. Watching her take what she needs from me, that turns me on even more.

Every little moan and whimper and gasp that comes out of her has sent a jolt straight to my cock. When her whole body tenses up and comes apart, hearing her call out my name sends me over the edge right with her. Sex with Astrid is a blast. I want to keep her up all night and see how many times I can get her to come before she begs me for mercy, but after going four rounds, and over a dozen orgasms, she can barely keep her eyes open. I'm spent too, for that matter.

We're lying together on the bed, Astrid facing away from me. I've got my body curled around her tight. She yawns and lifts her head off the pillow to look at the clock. It's after three in the morning, but I'm not ready for her to leave the bed.

"I should probably get going," she says over her shoulder.

"Will you stay? We could have wild shower sex in the morning." I try not to sound as desperate as I feel.

She hums. "I do like a good round of shower sex."

I tighten my arms around her, pressing her into me. "So, you'll stay then?" I give her shoulder a kiss.

"I'll stay, but only because I don't think I could make it back to my room if I wanted to."

I smile and press another kiss to her neck. "You're saying you enjoyed yourself, then?"

"If I say yes, will you let me go to sleep?" she says behind another yawn.

I laugh, untangling myself from her. "Give me one sec, don't fall asleep until I get back."

I close the blackout curtains and turn off all the lights. I climb back into bed and Astrid rolls over to face me.

"Come here," I say, pulling her against me.

She lays her head on my chest. I kiss the top of her head, inhaling the scent of her shampoo.

"Night, Cam," she mumbles. She's asleep in what seems like less than a minute.

I lie there awake for a while. I'm considering how I can convince Astrid to see me again. For a real date. I know next to nothing about her, but the season has, at most, four games left. Then I can spend the offseason wherever Astrid is. Plenty of guys have a second house where they spend the offseason. I can get a place close to her and we can see where this goes. I decide to tell her all about myself over coffee in bed in the morning. Hopefully, she's receptive to the idea of being in a relationship, and a long-distance one at that.

I don't remember falling asleep, but it's the best sleep I've gotten on the road in years. I don't even have any dreams, just deep, peaceful sleep.

A noise jolts me from the depths, though not enough to pull me all the way to the surface. I roll over, expecting to find Astrid, but I don't. I only find cool sheets. I sit up in the bed and only hear silence. Without even having to turn on the lights, I know Astrid is gone, taking with her any hope I had of seeing her again.

5

Cameron

Four Months Later

"Don't tell me you're still fixated on that girl from Vegas." Justin scoffs.

We're in the Bear's training facility for a team lifting session. After losing the Cup last season, I may have let myself spiral out of control. I spent hours scouring social media for Astrid and coming up empty. I might have also tried to bribe the hotel staff into giving me the personal details of the guests staying in Astrid's room. It got bad. Desperation is not a good look for me.

"Dude, I swear, I haven't thought about her in months." That is a total lie. I jerked off to the thought of her like three hours ago.

"Don't bullshit a bullshitter."

"Look man, I'm trying. It's a lot easier said than done." I haven't really tried all that hard.

"Answer one question for me." He crosses his arms over his chest. "If she were standing right here in front of you, right now, would you ask her out or walk away?"

Sighing, I resign myself to whatever shit he's going to dole out when I answer him. "Hands down, ask her out. Make her mine. I've never met a more perfect woman and I would do anything to be with her."

I can't help myself. I've tried everything to forget about her. I even went out with Justin and some other guys after the first away game with the sole intention of taking a bunny back to my hotel room. The guys, mainly Justin, convinced me I needed a palate cleanser, but I couldn't go through with it. I made up an excuse about why I wasn't feeling any of the girls at the bar that night and then ended up leaving early. The thought of taking someone else home just doesn't even interest me anymore. I want Astrid.

I've never had an interest in being in a relationship before. That's why I prefer no-strings-attached hookups while I'm out of town. My schedule during the season is packed with practices, training sessions, and traveling. I don't have time for relationships. In my experience, hooking up when I'm in town is too messy. Some women get the idea that if they sleep with me, I'll somehow want more. Hence, my away game only policy. It leaves no room for the possibility of tomorrow. I've never wanted that before. Not until I met Astrid.

Everything happens for a reason. But I'm struggling to come up with the reason for finding someone who was perfect in so many ways and being left with no way to reconnect with her. I suppose it's possible that I'm building her up in my mind. Maybe I'm putting her on a pedestal because I know there's no way I'll ever find her again.

Justin levels me with a look. “Is that why you kept the playoff beard? Because you think you might run into her on the street, and she won’t recognize you without the beard?” For once, he sounds sympathetic to me being hung up on Astrid.

“No, that’s not why I kept the playoff beard.”

He raises his eyebrows. “Oh, it’s not? What’s the reason, then?”

I struggle to come up with anything.

“That’s what I thought.” Justin looks satisfied.

“Listen, man.” I throw my hands up in exasperation. “I promise it’s not going to be a problem. Can we drop this already?”

In the first six games of the new season, we have been a force to be reckoned with. It’s early, but the team is working together the way we need to if we want to make a repeat appearance in the playoffs. After losing the Cup last season, we all want it that much more.

A few guys retired at the end of last season without realizing their dream of winning the Cup. I’m not sure how many more seasons I’ll be around. At twenty-nine, this is my ninth season in the NHL. There aren’t many starting centers who are in their thirties, and I’ve already noticed that my body doesn’t recover like it did in the early days of my career.

“I’ll drop it… If you promise to come out to the bar after the game Saturday and make an actual effort to forget about the girl from Vegas.”

I scoff, “I will if you promise to be my wingman.” For all the shit he gives me, Justin is a great guy.

He holds out a fist and I bump it. “You know I’m the best wingman of all time.”

6

Astrid

"Tyler asked me out again this morning," I say with a massive sigh.

"Oh, sweetie. Give that poor boy a break." Bailey pats my arm.

"Wait, I thought Tyler was married?" Mina says over the rim of her margarita.

"Nope, that's Corey. He got married last winter. Tyler is the one who always wears loafers because he thinks it makes him look sophisticated." Bailey loves making fun of Tyler.

"Not anymore, Corey got divorced. He's single again," Lori chimes in.

It's our weekly girls' night out. Every Wednesday, we leave work and head straight to a bar to catch up on all the hot gossip. You know those coworkers who become your best friends? That's Mina and Lori for me. Bailey has been my best friend since we were in elementary school. We've known each other long before we were ever coworkers.

Technically, Mina and Lori are in different departments than Bailey and me, but it's the same company so it counts. We all work for a huge marketing firm in Boston. Mina and

Lori work in accounting. I don't know how they look at numbers all day, every day. I sure as heck couldn't. Bailey is the head of public relations at our firm. That girl can seriously flip a script. I'm the head of graphic design. I get to design advertising campaigns all day and play with graphics, colors, fonts, you name it. I don't consider what I do—playing around on my tablet creating and designing—to be work. Staring at a spreadsheet of numbers all day, now that's work.

"What's the harm in going? He's nice enough, and I heard through the grapevine that he's got a big dick," Lori says nonchalantly.

"Lori, how do you know what size his dick is?" I raise my eyebrow at her.

She waves her hand. "I heard it from an eyewitness."

"I think you should bring that up to HR, to be honest," Mina says, laughing.

"I want to know how, in the course of normal office chatter, the subject came up." Bailey signals the waitress for another round.

"You had better not be ordering us tequila shots again! We agreed after last time that shots are reserved for weekends." I give her a glare.

"Relax," Bailey chides. "You don't have any meetings tomorrow morning. It's fine."

"The receptionist told me, by the way," Lori says, resting her chin on her hand.

We all gawk at her.

"What? She offered up the information when she heard he asked you out. Apparently, they used to date in college. I wouldn't be fulfilling my bestie duties if I didn't snoop a little bit."

I swear Lori could work for the CIA if she wanted to. Give that girl an internet connection and a name and she can find any information on anyone.

Except for Cameron. After Bailey and I got back from our trip to Las Vegas in June, I was pretty bummed that I didn't give him my number. Lori did her best to find him, but with only knowing his first name, there just wasn't enough to go on.

My disappointment was...unexpected. I knew going in it was a one-time-only deal, but by the time I was drifting off to sleep, something had shifted. At least for me it did. I fell asleep in his arms and for the first time in my life, it just felt right. Like I belonged there, tucked in tightly against him. I've never been able to sleep with anyone touching me, and that lack of physical closeness was one thing Landon cited as a contributing factor to his infidelity. Because clearly, it was my fault that he couldn't keep his dick in his pants.

Landon and I met in grad school. His family is quite wealthy, and to say the very least, he swept me off my feet. Made me feel like he was saving me or something. But Landon played some serious mind games on me. The kind of mind games that burn so slowly that you don't realize the impact they have on you until it's too late. The kind of mind games that make you forget who you are and what you're worth. I look back on it now as a blessing in disguise. I'll be honest, I don't think I really wanted to marry Landon, he just made me feel like it was my only option. It's seriously fucked up he ever got me to that mindset, but it didn't happen overnight. It was slow and deliberate. Calculated and timed perfectly to play on my insecurities and capitalize on my weaknesses. Financial security was the best thing he had going for him.

My dad died in a work accident just hours after I was born, leaving my mom on her own to raise three kids under the age of five. My mom has never remarried or even attempted to date again. We assure her that Dad would have wanted her to be happy and be taken care of, but she insists he was the only man she ever loved or would ever love. And she's carried that heartbreak with her all these years.

It definitely wasn't easy for her, raising three kids on her own. She and my dad were high school sweethearts. He was a senior when she was a sophomore. He gave up a football scholarship to stay in their hometown until she graduated and, in the meantime, got a job at a stamping plant. It paid good money and was a union job, and they had everything they ever wanted in each other. They had my sister a little over a year after being married.

My dad was my mom's whole world. Watching her carry the grief of losing him with her all these years is a pain worse than death. I can't imagine going through it myself. If I'm being completely honest, I was relieved when I walked in and found Landon in bed with his coworker. Because it meant I would be safe from that lifelong grief. The moment I realized I wasn't heartbroken, I remembered who I was. The fact that someone as pathetic as Landon made me forget is, frankly, embarrassing.

"Seriously, Astrid. It's time for you to get out and dip your toes in the water a bit." Mina's voice snaps me out of my thoughts.

"Exactly!" Bailey nods in agreement. "You can't hang out with us all the time. We all need the D, too."

I laugh, "Ok, fine. I'll go out with him. But I'm not getting my hopes up. I don't want it to be awkward at work."

The waitress sets down four tequila shots and we all glare at Bailey, who just grins back at us and picks up a shot.

"To Tyler's big dick!" Bailey calls out.

We all laugh as we clink our shot glasses together and down them. Thank God for good friends and good tequila.

***

"I am never drinking tequila again," I say from behind my sunglasses.

"You say that every time." Bailey hands me a coffee on our way into the elevator.

"Well, this time I mean it." The movement from the elevator is making my stomach churn. I fight back the urge to heave the whole way up to our marketing firm's floor.

Bailey just chuckles to herself as I push past her to make my way to my office. "Drink some water," she calls after me.

I sit at my desk, wondering why I didn't just call in sick. Because I'm usually good after I rehydrate and eat something, that's why. And I'm a grown-ass woman, I can own up to my mistakes. No one forced me to take four tequila shots at the bar last night. At least I think it was only four. Things got blurry fast after the third, and I only remember flashes after the fourth.

A voice drifts into my office from down the hall. Oh no. I can't deal with this right now.

"Astrid!" Tyler's voice booms as he appears in the doorway of my office. "Got plans Saturday night? I've got Bears tickets and I'd love to take you." He plops down in the chair across from my desk.

"If I agree, will you use a whisper to communicate with me until after lunch?" I rub my aching temples.

"I take it girls' night went well then?" Tyler knows all about our Wednesday night rituals, though they usually don't result in Thursday morning hangovers.

"Are we communicating solely in questions now?" I'm too nauseous for this.

"Does that mean you'll go out with me?" He flashes a perfect smile.

Tyler *is* cute, and Bailey's right, he's nice enough. At least he is at work. I have no idea what he's like outside the office. I blow out a breath, hoping I don't live to regret this decision. "Yes, I'll go out with you."

"Great," he says. "Do you want to meet me at TD Garden or for me to pick you up?"

"Whatever is easiest for you."

"I'll pick you up at six. See you then, gorgeous." He gives me a big smile on his way out of my office.

I spend the rest of my morning fighting for my life against this hangover. After a couple cups of coffee and some ibuprofen, I feel a little better. Bailey and I order burgers and fries for lunch, which takes away the last of the effects of the tequila from last night.

"Are you excited for Saturday?" she asks me between huge bites of her burger.

I nod, chewing. "I am, actually. It's been a while since I've been on a first date, but I'm looking forward to it." I'm also very nervous about it.

"I'm happy for you, girlie." Bailey smiles at me and squeezes my hand. "You deserve a guy who treats you right. I hope Tyler can be that person for you."

I smile back. "I do, too." I really hope he is.

The rest of the work week passes quickly. I spend Saturday morning cleaning my apartment on the off chance I want to invite Tyler back to my place. It's been a bit of a dry spell for me, and while the old Astrid wouldn't normally have sex on the first date, the new Astrid isn't going to rule it out. Or, if we're talking about Vegas Astrid, there's no need for the date at all.

It doesn't take me long to clean at all. My apartment is only about five hundred square feet, but it's cute, it's mine, and I love it. It's in Somerville, slightly north of Boston, and only about a half mile away from the Green Line T station at

Gilman Square. My building is an old, three-story Victorian duplex that was remodeled into six smaller apartments. My unit is nestled on the second floor, and I got lucky with my neighbors. The guy who lives above me works nights, so I hardly ever see or hear him when I'm home. The first floor is occupied by an elderly couple that have been married for some crazy long amount of time. They are so sweet and treat me like one of their grandkids.

When I'm satisfied that my apartment is the right balance of clean yet lived-in, I shower, straighten my hair, and put on some light makeup. Nothing too crazy, just a light smokey eye and neutral lip, just a little darker than what I do during the week for work. I put on a pair of tight skinny jeans, a warm, oversized sweater, and some cute ankle boots.

My doorbell rings right at six. I'm kind of impressed with Tyler's punctuality and I wonder if he's been sitting at the curb waiting out the clock. He greets me with a quick peck on the cheek, and when we get to the car, he opens the car door for me.

"You look great, Astrid," he says as he slides in behind the wheel.

"So," I hedge, uncomfortable with the compliment, "what did you do today?"

"Oh, you know, just hung out. How about you?"

Are first dates always this awkward? "Pretty much the same."

I regret leaving the decision to spend an extra thirty minutes in the car up to Tyler. We already know all the typical first date information about each other from being coworkers, but we are nowhere near the stage of discussing what we want for our futures. At least we won't have to talk too much during the game, I hope. I don't actually know what attending a hockey game is like.

"So," he says, clearly feeling the same awkwardness as I am. "Have you ever been to a Bears game?"

"I have not. I've wanted to ever since moving here, just never had the opportunity to make it happen."

"I know how that goes." He lets out an awkward laugh and our conversation stalls out again.

Thirty minutes later, we're finding our way to our seats.

"Oh my God, Tyler, these seats are fantastic!" I'm super impressed. We're sitting center ice, only a few rows back from the penalty box.

He gives me a sly grin. "Glad you like them."

"You didn't have to go all out on these tickets, you know. I would've been fine to sit on the second level" I feel a little guilty. These seats are way better than what the quality of our date warrants, thus far.

Tyler waves me off. "It's not a big deal. A family friend has season tickets. They're in the Bahamas this week, so they offered their tickets to me."

So, clearly his family has some connections. "These are awesome seats. You'll have to tell them thank you for me."

The players from both teams are on the ice warming up. It's hard to even focus on a single player as they skate in big circles and figure eights. Meanwhile, the Jumbotron shows player stats, interviews, and highlights.

"I'm going to go grab a beer before the first period. Want anything?"

"Sure, I'll take a beer." I get up to follow Tyler to the concession stand, but he waves me down.

"I'll go, you stay here." He leans in and gives me a kiss on the cheek. He winks at me again. "Be right back."

I feel awkward while Tyler is gone. I don't really enjoy being in public spaces by myself. When the Zamboni comes out to clean the ice before the game starts, I have even less distraction from being alone. I pull out my phone and start scrolling Instagram when a text pops up in our girls' group chat.

Bailey: How's the big date??

Me: Awkward... I don't really know what to talk about with him

"Not at all."

I hope he didn't see what I was typing. I take a sip, hoping the alcohol will put me at ease and make the conversation a bit more natural.

The stadium goes dark for the home team to make their big entrance. Tyler and I drink and cheer for each of the Bears' players. The announcer calls out the name of Boston's captain and as I tip my pint glass up to take a drink, my eyes catch a look at the player's picture as it flashes across the Jumbotron. As soon as I see him, I forget how to drink. My beer goes down my airway and I cough into the glass, sending a splash of liquid down my shirt. I continue coughing while a very concerned Tyler whacks me on the back, asking if I'm okay.

"I'll go grab you some napkins." He jumps up and is in the aisle on his way back to the concession stand before I've even caught my breath.

Cameron's face is gone by the time I look up at the screen again. I search the faces of the players lining up on the ice for the national anthem, but still can't spot him. I take out my phone and quickly text the group chat.

Me: OH MY FUCKING GOD YOU GUYS
Me: HE'S A HOCKEY PLAYER

Bailey: Who's a hockey player?

Mina: I didn't know Tyler played hockey?

Me: NO
Me: CAMERON!!
Me: HE PLAYS FOR THE FUCKING BEARS!!!!!!!!!!

Lori: OMG!!!
Lori: CJ GRANT! C FOR CAMERON!
Lori: I should have thought of that!

I frantically search the ice for him, but I didn't catch what his number was before the screen switched over to the next player. I type the name Lori just sent, CJ Grant, into Google. Immediately, my screen fills with pictures of my Las Vegas Mystery Man. Star center and captain of the Boston Bears.

Bailey: HOLY MOTHER FUCKING SHIT BALLS
Bailey: ASTRID
Bailey: YOU FUCKED AN NHL PLAYER
Bailey: I HAVE NEVER BEEN MORE PROUD OF YOU!!!!

Tyler returns with a pile of napkins, and I pocket my phone. I look down when he holds out the napkins to me, and realize that when I sloshed my drink, I got half my upper left thigh wet. I blot at the stain on my jeans, hoping that I don't reek of beer as it dries.

"Are you okay?" Tyler asks.

"Uh, yeah. I'm good." I hope I at least sound convincing. Internally, I'm freaking out.

He gives me a sidelong look. Clearly, he's not convinced. I must look as frazzled as I feel.

By now, the game is underway. My eyes are locked on Cam. He speeds down the ice in a flash, maneuvering easily past the other team's defense and flipping the puck into the net in a blur. My insides turn to mush watching him. I would have never pegged him as a professional athlete in Las Vegas based on his personality, but it does explain his insane stamina. Just thinking about all the orgasms he gave me is giving me butterflies.

I know next to nothing about hockey, but it's clear that the game is physically intense. Cam and the other team's center seem to slam each other into the boards every chance they get.

"Come on, that was slashing!" Tyler yells, then leans in as if I couldn't hear him. "These refs are blind."

I just nod in agreement because I don't know what that means, and I didn't see anything that seemed any more violent than what seems to be the baseline for the game.

On the next play, Cam and the other team's center get caught against the boards and the referees frantically blow their whistles. The whole arena erupts in boos as one referee explains the call and another escorts Cam over toward the penalty box. The butterflies take flight again when I realize that in just a few seconds, the mysterious love machine from Vegas that I've been obsessing over for the last four months will be a stone's throw away.

The referee closes the door to the penalty box behind Cam, and before he takes a seat, he glances up into the stands. Our eyes lock and my heart jumps into my throat. Cam stands frozen in place, a look of disbelief on his face. For an instant, the arena is silent, and the only sound reaching my ears is the sound of my own heart pounding in my chest. I see recognition flash across Cam's features, followed by something else—relief, maybe?—and he turns to sit on the bench.

"Well, that was weird." Tyler's voice pulls me back to Earth. "Do you like... know him or... something?"

Shit. I was hoping he hadn't seen that.

"Uh, yeah..." I have no idea how to tell my date that yes, I have in fact seen the captain of his favorite NHL team naked.

"It seems like there might be a story or something there," Tyler hedges.

As I take a calming breath to steady myself, Tyler elbows me and points up to the screen. I'm mortified to see Tyler and myself framed by a heart. I don't have time to process that we're on the kiss cam, and as I turn to explain how I know Cam, Tyler closes the distance and plasters his lips to mine. The crowd cheers and claps, but this is the least romantic or enjoyable kiss I've ever had.

Tyler turns back to the game, instantly engrossed as Boston is trying to prevent the other team from scoring while being down a player. I glance back at the penalty box to see Cam's eyes locked back on me, looking absolutely feral. The buzzer signals the end of his penalty time and Cam rushes back out onto the ice.

Another minute goes by, and Cam goes back to the bench along with two other players as three new players zoom past them onto the ice. I watch Cam from across the arena. I can't tell for sure, due to the distance, but it looks like he's motioning over toward the penalty box. Then the two other players' eyes lock onto me. I feel my cheeks flame and try to force myself to focus on the game, but the only thing I can think about is Cam's naked body and all the wild sex we had in Vegas. When the players leave the ice at the end of the first period, I finally feel like I can breathe again.

"Hey." Tyler turns to me. "Would you want to go grab a bite to eat after this? There's a bar right down the street that has really good food and usually some players show up after home games."

Before I can stop myself or change my mind, I give Tyler a big smile. "I'd like that."

7

Cameron

Everything happens for a reason. I can't contain my smile as we walk down the chute to the locker room at the end of the first period.

"So, that's really her?" Justin asks me as we take our seats in the locker room.

I give him a grin. "It's her."

"Who's that she's with?" he asks.

I shake my head. "Man, I have no idea, but I don't like him."

"I'm pretty sure I know who it is."

Our heads swivel over to the newest player on the team, Reid. He was just drafted from the NCAA at the start of the season. At twenty years old, he's one of the youngest players on the team. But the kid is a beast and definitely holds his own on the ice.

"I'm pretty sure he's one of the regulars at Mac's." Reid shrugs.

"Mac's?" I have no idea what he's talking about.

"The bunny bar, dude, keep up." Justin would know.

"Pretty sure it's the same guy. I've seen him over there after every game so far," he adds.

I let my smile creep back. "Justin, you still up for being my wingman tonight?"

Justin lets out a whoop and goes to give me a high five before Coach comes in and shuts us all up.

The second period gets underway and not two minutes in, Chicago has scored a goal and tied up the game. Every time my line gets called back for a shift change, my eyes wander over to Astrid. The guy she's with looks like a total douche. I am man enough to admit I'm jealous. I wish I had been the one to get onto the kiss cam with her. Though from where I sat, it sure didn't look like she was into the kiss. That's a good sign for me.

The third period passes in a similar fashion. Every time I'm off the ice, my gaze is locked on Astrid. During the last few minutes of the game, the center for Chicago corners me again, saying something shitty, and again I lose my temper. The referee escorts me to the sin bin yet again, and I throw myself down on the bench. Funny how they keep calling me on late hits when Chicago's center has been charging me all night and has not been called once.

I turn around on the bench and watch Astrid and the douchebag. He's got his scrawny little arm around her, talking loudly into her ear. She looks totally uninterested in whatever it is he's saying. I can't hide my smile when she catches me staring at her.

She looks different than she did in Vegas. Her brown hair is straightened and hangs down past her shoulders.

She's wearing heavier make up than what I saw her wear last summer. I have a million questions for her. Why did she walk out? How is she here? Did she feel all the air get sucked out of the arena when we locked eyes like I did? What's her fucking last name and phone number?

When my penalty is up, I hit the ice hard. The score is still tied at one to one, and we only have seconds left to make a play. I have no desire to let this game go into overtime. My focus is to win this and then hope to God that douche drags Astrid to the bar he apparently goes to after every game.

Justin and I charge Chicago's defense, tricking them both into covering us while Reid breaks away with the puck. As I come around the back of the net, Reid flicks the puck to me, just like their goalie expects. What he doesn't expect, though, is for Justin to be back in front of the net. As soon as the puck connects with my stick, I send it flying to Justin, who flicks it easily past the goalie, the buzzer going off half a second later, and we win the game.

I'm showered and dressed in record time after the game. I'm obligated to give some attention to the media as I'm leaving the locker room. Talking to the media is the least enjoyable part of my job. Lucky for me, Justin is the one they want to talk to tonight, since he scored the game-winning goal. When he's finished answering questions, we make our way down the street to Mac's pub.

"So, what's the plan?" Justin asks. "How are you going to get her to leave with you?"

I level him with a glare. “I’m not going to try to get her to leave with me.”

“Why the hell not, man? You’ve been fantasizing about her since June.”

“Mainly because I need to convince her to go on a real date with me first.” I hold the door and let him walk in ahead of me.

Justin shakes his head in disbelief. “Why would you want to do that?”

I’m not in the mood to explain myself to him, a giant manwhore. I doubt he’d understand that I want to do this right. “Let’s just get some drinks and hope that she’s here.”

We make our way over to the bar through the crowded dining room. It’s been a long time since I’ve been out to a bar after a home game. While we wait for the bartender to make his rounds, Justin takes out his phone.

“Oh sweet, Reid and the guys have a table in the back.” He turns to scan the crowd and I find myself looking for Astrid, disappointment seeping into my mood when I don’t see her.

Justin orders four pitchers of beer for the table, and we weave through the crowd to the back. When we find the rest of the guys, it’s pretty clear they’ve had a head start. Empty shot glasses and pitchers litter the table along with half-eaten baskets of fries and nachos. There are a few bunnies mingling with my teammates, all vying for someone to take them home for the night.

I take a seat at one end of the table and a pretty waitress approaches with a tray piled high with more food. From where I'm sitting, I have a pretty good view of the entire bar. There are still throngs of people pouring in, but I haven't seen Astrid. I decide I might as well make the most of being here, so I join in the conversation happening around me. Before I know it, the four pitchers of beer Justin and I had ordered are empty and he's making his way back from the bar with four more.

"Hey, Grant!" he calls out as he approaches the table. "Look who I ran into. This is Tyler, he's a big fan of yours."

I recognize the guy on Justin's heels as the douche who was all over Astrid at the game. I look over his shoulder, expecting to find her, but he seems to be alone.

"Hey man, nice to meet you," I lie.

I'm more than a little annoyed that he may not have made sure Astrid got home safe. He seems pretty buzzed. Maybe that means their date didn't go so well. I wonder if I can talk him into giving me Astrid's address and I can swing by... No. I push the thought away. That's too much.

Tyler starts to talk about typical fan stuff. I'm suddenly not in the mood to be out in public anymore. I excuse myself to go to the bathroom, planning on making my escape and going home. I scan the crowd as I walk toward the bathroom, but again, I don't see Astrid. She must have gone home instead of tagging along with Douchebag to the bar after the game. Another chance with Astrid gone, just like that.

Now that my mood is thoroughly soured, it's time for me to leave. I type out a quick text to Justin instead of fighting the crowd to get back to the table. I'm looking down at my phone as I round a corner and slam into someone. The blow nearly knocks the poor woman off her feet as she bounces off my chest, but I manage to grab her elbow and steady her.

She starts apologizing profusely as she brushes the hair out of her face. Relief floods me as her eyes finally land on mine.

"Hi, Astrid." I forgot how drop-dead gorgeous she is up close. And she smells amazing, like coconut and something fruity.

"Cameron. Hi," she says, surprised.

"You're here. In Boston."

She nods, taking half a step away from me. "I am."

"What brings you to town? Please tell me you're not just here for the weekend."

She smiles. "I live here, actually."

Oh, thank fuck. I let out a puff of air and I can't stop the enormous grin from spreading across my face. "So that means there's a chance, then?"

Her brows knit together. "A chance for what?"

"For me to take you out on a date." I flash her my trademark smile. The one that melts the panties off any woman with a pulse. Funnily enough, though, I hadn't thought to use it on her in Vegas.

She looks down at her feet. “I’d really like to but—”

“That sounds like a no.” I clutch my hand to my heart, feigning heartbreak. “What can I do to change your mind?”

She shakes her head, but her gaze is locked on my mouth. She looks like she’s trying to find the right words to say no again, so I speak up before she can.

“Astrid.” I reach for her hand and she looks down at the point we’re joined before meeting my gaze. “At least come talk to me for a minute. You owe me that much after disappearing on me in Vegas.”

She blows out a breath. “It was good to see you again, but I can’t. I’m here with someone, on a date, if you can call it that? I don’t know, he’s a coworker, and he’s been asking me out for like the last three months, so I finally decided to go out with him and now I can’t find him.”

God, I forgot how she rambles when she’s flustered. It’s adorable. “I think I know where he’s at, actually.”

She looks surprised. “You do?”

“Yeah, Justin, one of my teammates, invited him to join us. We’ve got a table in the back.”

“Ah, right. Your teammate. Because you’re a professional hockey player.” She lets out a small laugh. “Wow, I literally know nothing about you.”

“Well then, come have a drink with me and we can fix that.” It’s taking all my willpower not to put my hands all over her and do the things I’ve fantasized about doing with her since our night together in Vegas.

"A drink?"

Was that disappointment I heard in her voice? I rake my eyes over her: her breathing is heavy, pupils dilated, cheeks flushed. Oh yeah. She's just as affected by our proximity as I am. I like knowing I have that effect on her. Maybe it was disappointment I heard. In which case... *Screw willpower.*

"Or, if you'd like to, we can get out of here and have some real fun."

"That's a bold assumption to make," she scoffs.

I lean down to speak softly into her ear, trying not to get lost in the overwhelming sensation of being so close to her. "If you've thought about that night even a fraction as much as I have, then I'd say it's a *safe* assumption to make." I pull back so we're speaking at a normal distance again. "Then again, since you're here with someone, I won't keep you. How is the date going, by the way?"

She gives me an annoyed glare. "It's going fine."

I grimace. "Ouch, do you want to tell him, or should I?"

"Tell him what?"

"That there won't be a second date." I grin.

She swats my arm. "Cameron."

I grab my arm, pretending like the hit hurt. "Don't tell me you're going out with him again," I groan.

"He hasn't asked me yet. Why do you care?"

"Because I want you to go out with me."

"And what makes you think I'm interested?" She squares her shoulders in challenge, but I caught the quick falter in her resolve.

"For one, you're over here talking to me instead of going to find your date. Two, you keep looking at my mouth, so I know you're thinking about kissing me." I smirk and lean in close to speak against the shell of her ear, this time resting my hand on the curve of her hip. "And three, your pupils just dilated to the size of saucers when I mentioned kissing."

Her chest rises as she draws in a breath.

I drop my hand and straighten up to my full height. "But, since you are here on a date, let's go find your man."

"He is not my man!"

"Even better," I chuckle.

8

Astrid

Because I want you to go out with me. Cameron's words echo in my head as we weave through the crowd back to his table. I can feel his heated touch on my lower back, even through my sweater. The butterflies in my stomach are replaced with a pang of guilt when I catch sight of Tyler.

"Astrid!" Tyler says way too loud when he sees our approach. He throws an arm over my shoulder, putting too much of his weight on me and nearly throwing me off balance. Clearly, he's drunk. I wonder how that happened so fast because ten minutes ago, he just seemed slightly buzzed.

"I want you to meet my new friends," Tyler slurs directly into my ear. "This is Justin. And these are the rest of the guys."

I feel Cameron watching me, which throws me off balance nearly as much as Tyler's weight on my shoulder. I move to free myself from this half-hug situation. Tyler drops his arm and I feel a sense of victorious relief for a brief moment until he puts his arm right back on my shoulder and that feeling is replaced by defeat.

"Hi." I wave to everyone. The one named Justin looks familiar. He might have been one of the guys from the lobby at Mandalay Bay when I first saw Cam.

We join them at the table, me across from Cameron and Tyler next to me. He throws his arm over the back of my chair and my level of comfort with this situation plummets. I feel so out of place surrounded by ten incredibly attractive men who are, in turn, surrounded by some very attractive women who eye me with suspicion. Everyone goes back to their various conversations, which all seem to happen around me.

Cameron isn't engaging in conversation with the others, either. He's just watching me with a heated stare. I'd like to talk to him about what happened in Las Vegas, but not here in front of everyone. Especially not in front of Tyler, who keeps pounding the beer and is getting increasingly handsy, despite me pushing his hand away every time it ends up on my thigh. This night is quickly gaining "worst first date" status.

I look over at Cameron. His jaw is clenched, fury radiating off his broad frame. Justin leans over to say something in Cam's ear, and he nods. They both stand and come around to our side of the table.

Justin claps Tyler on the back, who stands as well. "Hey man, it was great hanging out with you, but I think you should probably head home and get some rest."

Tyler turns to me. "You ready to head out? I'll give you a ride."

I open my mouth to tell him I'll find my own way home, but Justin beats me to it.

"We'll make sure she gets home safe. Come on, let's get you an Uber." He claps a massive hand on his shoulder, turns him around, and marches him toward the front of the bar.

Surprisingly, he goes willingly. I might be offended at being left alone at a bar if I also weren't so relieved.

Cam leans down to speak close to my ear. "You should stay for a bit. Give him a chance to leave."

I nod before I can really think about it. I'll use the excuse of waiting until Tyler has left to stay and have the conversation I need to have with Cam. "Yeah, I was kind of hoping we could talk?"

His eyebrows shoot up. "Yeah, absolutely." He signals the waitress and asks her if we can get a booth.

We follow the waitress over to a different section of the bar and get what seems to be the only empty table in the place.

"Can I get you anything?" The waitress directs the question to Cam.

"I'll take another beer," I say to her, smiling.

She turns to me and presses her lips into a line. "Sure," she says dryly before turning back to Cam and plastering on a saccharine smile. "Anything for you?"

My eyes go from her to Cam. I'm expecting him to be looking up at her since she just asked him a question, but he's looking at me instead.

He smirks. "I'll take a beer, too," he replies without dropping my gaze.

We sit in silence watching one another, waiting for the waitress to drop off our drinks. She must grab the bottles from the bar herself because she's back in record time. She pops the cap off one bottle, sets it neatly down in front of Cam, and gives him a smile. She repeats the process for the second bottle, only she sets down a little too roughly in front of me, without smiling.

When she leaves us again, a smile creeps onto Cameron's face. "Jealousy looks good on you, Astrid," he says around his beer bottle.

"Yeah, okay." I take a drink, trying to hide the fact that he caught me red-handed.

He slaps his hands down on the table. "So, what did you want to talk about?"

"Well, mainly, I wanted to explain why I left in Vegas." I wring my hands. I'm not sure why I'm so nervous.

"Astrid, it's fine." He puts up a hand to stop me. "You don't have to explain yourself. We both knew going into it that it was a one-night thing and that's exactly what happened."

I take a deep breath, trying to calm my nerves. "I don't typically do the whole one-night thing. I was in a bad place mentally and I'm not proud of the way I handled things."

His face drops. "So, you regret it then."

"I don't regret sleeping with you. I regret that I left abruptly and without saying goodbye. I realized I handled it poorly as soon as I was on the plane back to Boston. I'm sorry."

He reaches across the table and takes my hand. "Thank you for the apology, but it's not necessary." He looks at me thoughtfully before releasing my hand and taking a sip of his beer. "But since you seem so torn up about it, there is something you could do to make it up to me."

"Cam, I am not sleeping with you again." But damn, I wouldn't say no if he asked me twice. Although now that he knows I live here in Boston, I don't want to get put on what I'm sure is a rotating roster of women he calls up when he's in the mood for a quick fuck.

He lets out a low laugh. "No, that's not what I'm talking about, though I wouldn't turn it down."

"Alright, what is it then?" I chuckle behind my beer. This ought to be good.

"Go on a date with me." He speaks softly, holding my gaze.

That is not what I was expecting him to say, and butterflies soar in my stomach. I want to say no. I want to tell him that tonight was supposed to be a fun way for me to get back out there into the dating world. I want to tell him that my utter lack of chemistry with Tyler makes me want to turn right back around and never set foot outside my cozy apartment again. But I also want to say yes.

Cameron breaks the silence of my indecision. "Astrid, you aren't the only one who has regrets about that night." A smirk breaks free at one corner of his mouth. "Hell, I tried to bribe the hotel staff to give me your information."

I pause, my beer an inch away from my lips. "You did what?"

He laughs. "I may have gone a little crazy trying to find any information I could on you. I offered the resort staff an embarrassing amount of money. They could not be persuaded. Obviously, I would have called if they had."

I blink at him. "That might be the most..." I don't know how to label this, honestly.

"Desperate thing you've ever heard?" he offers and laughs.

"I was going to say 'romantic' but yeah, desperate works, too." I can't help but smile around him. "They would have given you Bailey's number, though. She was the one who booked the room. My name wasn't on the reservation at all."

He nods before a grin spreads across his face. "So, is that a yes, then?"

I sigh, trying to mask the fact that this is a no-brainer for me. "Yes, Cameron. I will go on a date with you."

He pumps his fist in victory and I laugh.

"You know, I tried to find you too," I say quietly.

"You did?" He cocks a brow.

"Well, not me. My friend, Lori, did. I swear she could work for the CIA. Not that I was trying to stalk you or anything," I tack on.

The corner of his mouth quirks up into a smile. "What did she find?"

"Absolutely nothing," I say, laughing. "It was actually a bit of a blow to her ego. She spiraled a little. But we had no idea that you were a hockey player—"

"And I use my initials in my career," he finishes.

I nod and take another drink. "Why is that, by the way?"

He stiffens slightly and takes a deep breath. "CJ was always what my grandpa called me. He passed away the day before I got drafted into the NHL, and it was my way to honor his memory." He takes a long sip of beer.

I reach across the table and squeeze his hand. "I'm so sorry. It sounds like you were close."

He sighs, nodding. "Him and my grandma took care of me a lot when I was little. My mom was a single mother and she had me young. I don't ever remember a time when she wasn't working, to be honest." For a moment, he has a faraway look in his eyes. Then he snaps out of it and looks back at me. "But it all worked out. She met my stepdad when I was four and within two years, they had two more kids together, my sisters. My stepdad is a great guy, and he gave my mom the kind of life she deserved to have from the start."

"That's great." I pause, but curiosity wins out. "And what about your dad?"

He blows out a breath. "He bailed before my mom even knew she was pregnant. My stepdad tried to track him down and get him to have some part of my life when I was in high school, but he wasn't interested. I've only spoken to him a handful of times and I have no interest in a relationship with him at this point."

"That's rough. I'm sorry." I give him a half smile.

He shrugs and takes another sip of his beer. Tipping his chin toward me, he says, "What about you? Are your parents still together?"

I shift uncomfortably and pick at the label on my bottle of beer. "Uh no, my dad passed away when I was a baby."

When I look back up at Cameron, I'm expecting to be met with the same regret-filled look I've seen a thousand times. But he's not looking at me like he's imagining all the years of grief I must have dealt with. Instead, his steady gaze is encouraging me to continue.

"My parents were high school sweethearts." I let out a half laugh, remembering the story I've heard a thousand times. "My dad got a good union factory job and made enough money to support my mom while she went to nursing school. My oldest sister was born less than a year after my mom started working as a trauma nurse at the county hospital, then my brother was born the following year. And me another year after that.

"Their plan was for my mom to stay home with all three of us kids after I was born. My dad was working a bunch of overtime to save up some money to make the transition a little easier. He got a call from his supervisor asking if he could come in and cover a shift the day after I was born. My mom was still in the hospital with me, my siblings were with our grandparents, so they decided that the overtime pay was worth it, and he wouldn't be missing much.

"He had been gone for only a couple of hours, and I'm not exactly sure what happened. My mom doesn't like to talk about it. But he got hurt on the job and they brought him to the same hospital my mom worked at and was in the maternity ward at the time. One of the emergency room doctors came up to her room with a couple of the other nurses to tell her. At the time, she apparently thought they were just coming up to congratulate her. My grandma told me when I was a teenager that she refused to believe them when they told her he had died and just went on as if he was going to walk back through the door any minute."

I blink back the sting of tears, willing them to dry up. "So, in an instant, she became a twenty-four-year-old widow with three kids."

Cam regards me with an almost wistful look and shakes his head. "I can't even imagine how difficult that must have been."

I take a long drink of my beer. "The only saving grace is that the union forced the factory to pay out his full pension on top of the life insurance he had, so there was never really anything my mom ever had to worry about, at least with respect to the loss of his income. His pension still gets paid out monthly."

"Wow," he says. "Do your siblings remember him?"

"My sister has a couple memories of him, but she says they're fuzzy. Mostly, she remembers the aftermath of his death. My brother doesn't remember him at all."

"That's awful. I'm sorry you all had to go through that." Cam gives me a sincere look that doesn't make me feel sorry for myself.

I shrug. "I never knew anything different. The grief was such a part of our life that it felt normal, if that makes any sense."

He nods, "It does, actually." I can tell he's speaking from his own experience.

Cameron is the first person I've talked to about my family that hasn't made me feel like a victim of my own life's circumstances. It's somehow comforting and unsettling all at the same time and I'm worried if I let myself get used to it, I'll be disappointed when it all inevitably gets taken away.

I have my mind made up to leave when the waitress stops by a moment later.

"I should get going. If I stay for another drink, I might end up doing something reckless, like sleeping with a pro athlete." I smile mischievously.

"Well in that case, let me get the next round," Cam pretends to signal back the waitress.

I laugh as I scoot to the edge of the booth's bench. "Oh, did you think I meant you? I was talking about Justin." And with that, I make a clean getaway to the door while Cameron is left sitting in stunned silence.

9

Cameron

This woman has a mouth on her. I finally recover and rush to catch up to Astrid before she can run away from me. Again. She's fast, I'll give her that. With her being significantly smaller than I am, she easily weaves her way through the crowded bar.

I finally burst through the door and nearly trip over a group of girls taking selfies on the sidewalk. I search the mostly empty street, but she's gone. *Dammit.* How does she keep doing this?

I consider rejoining my teammates but decide against it and head back toward the parking garage at the arena. How the hell did I not even think to ask for her number again? I didn't even get any information about her I can use to find her. *Again.* Sure, she knows how to find me, especially now that she knows I go by CJ professionally. A quick Google search will yield both personal social media accounts as well as professional accomplishments. But for some reason, I lost my ability to think clearly and have the foresight to ask Astrid what her last name was. *Again.*

The next morning comes entirely too fast. I'm not used to going out to the bars after games anymore. I need a solid eight hours to sleep and recover after game nights. Gone are the days of closing down the bars and getting a whopping two hours of sleep before having to be up and on the ice for practice. Unfortunately, last night was closer to the latter, and I'm feeling the difference in my energy as I go through my routine of getting geared up for practice.

"Good morning, sunshine!" Justin is entirely too chipper as he sits down on the locker room bench next to me. "You left in a rush last night. Any chance the reason you're so sluggish this morning has to do with a certain person whose name rhymes with Smastrid?"

"No," I say curtly, hoping he'll take the hint and drop it.

"No? What happened?"

I glare at him. "She disappeared on me."

Justin's eyebrows shoot up. "Again? No, you know what? I'm not surprised."

"You're an asshole," I say dryly.

"Oh, come on, don't be like that. You should be thanking me."

"For what?" I say, scowling at him.

"Because," he smirks, "I am the best wingman of all time. That's what." He pokes me in the chest.

"And what exactly does that mean? Because yet again, I'm left with no way of getting in touch with her." I'm too tired to play these games with him.

"That dude she was with last night was her *coworker*." He puts emphasis on the last word, like it will make his muddled meaning clearer.

I shrug. "What's that got to do with anything?" This is getting obnoxious.

"I thought you might have trouble sealing the deal with her last night, so I decided to build in an insurance policy." He looks like he's choosing his words carefully.

"I swear if you took bets on whether or not I could get a girl to give me a blow job in the bar bathroom, *again*, I will kill you." That isn't something I'm proud of. I got head in the bathroom of a bar once during my rookie year. I was pretty drunk and don't remember the details, but from the way Justin tells the story, I had some serious game.

His head falls back in laughter. "Oh my god, dude, I had totally forgotten about that!"

I sit staring at him for several minutes while he continues to laugh his ass off at the memory. Just as I'm getting ready to deck him, he finally composes himself.

"Oh man, thanks for that. I gotta remember to tell Reid about that one." He takes a deep breath and wipes the tears from the corner of his eyes. He claps me on the back. "You may not have the game you once did, but I sure as shit do."

My anger flares. Astrid wouldn't give him her number, would she? I thought she was joking last night about Justin, but now I'm not so sure. "Justin, you are fucking dead to me if you so much as breathed in Astrid's direction last night."

"What? Fuck no, man. Why would you think that?" His confusion seems genuine, then realization dawns on him. "Oh, because of the game thing? No."

I close my eyes, trying like hell to find some patience. "Get to the fucking point."

"I got *Tyler's* number," he says victoriously.

I stare at him, waiting for him to continue, but he doesn't. He just stares back at me with a dumb grin plastered across his face.

"Am I missing something here?"

"Jesus, dude." He huffs. "I texted him this morning. Made up a lie about her leaving something at the bar and asked if I could have her contact info to get it back to her. He gave me Astrid's number to give to you."

"Tyler gave you Astrid's number to give to me." I'm stunned.

"Yes." He looks at me expectantly.

"You have Astrid's number?"

"Yes, we've established that." He reaches into his pocket and holds out a small piece of paper to me. "Here you go, call her now if you don't believe me."

I look at the numbers scrolled across the paper. "This is Astrid's number." A huge grin spreads across my face.

"Yes. You're welc—"

I grab Justin and pull him into a bear hug. "Thank you, man. Seriously, you have no idea—"

He pushes me away. "I know. Just don't blow it, alright? And don't let this be a distraction."

I don't waste any time. I pull my phone out and punch in the numbers.

Me: Your disappearing act is almost as impressive as it is offensive to my confidence

Astrid: ....?
Astrid: Who is this?
Astrid: Cameron? How did you get my number?

Me: Tyler gave Justin your number and I just got it from him
Me: I'm headed into practice, but can I call you after?

Astrid: Yeah, I guess?

Morning skate drags on for what feels like hours. Well, it is actually two hours, but it seems like a lot longer. As soon as Coach dismisses us, I head for the showers and get dressed. I'm out the door before half of my teammates are even finished getting out of their gear.

I dig my phone out of my pocket while I'm walking to the car. Astrid picks up on the third ring.

"Hey." Her warm voice brings a smile to my face.

"Well, if it isn't little Miss Houdini herself." I slide into my SUV and start it up, waiting for the Bluetooth to pick up the call over the car's speakers.

Astrid's lilting laugh fills the leather interior as if she's sitting right beside me. "Well, it didn't take you as long to track me down this time as it did before."

"Track *you* down? I wasn't the one to show up to your game with another guy to try to make me jealous."

"Aww, are you intimidated by Tyler?" she coos.

"Definitely not."

"Uh-huh. Keep telling yourself that. Speaking of Tyler, remind me to kick him in the nuts for handing out my number to complete strangers."

I laugh. "Oh, come on, he wouldn't have had to if you hadn't disappeared on me. Again."

"You got me there."

"What are you doing tonight?"

The question slips out before I can think of a better way to frame it. Hearing her laugh makes me miss the sight of her smile. I need to see her again.

"Why do you ask?"

"What do you mean, why? Our date." I hope she hasn't changed her mind. "I was hoping I could take you out to dinner."

"I can't, I've got a situation I'm helping a friend with. What about next weekend?"

"No, that's too long. How about tomorrow?"

She laughs. "Too long? It's five days away."

"Yeah, and that's five days too many." I can't let Astrid slip through my fingers again, and I feel like the sooner I can get her to go out with me, the less likely she is to run. "And besides that, we leave on Tuesday for a few away games."

"I can make tomorrow work." I hear the smile in her voice.

"Yeah?" I feel my own smile break out.

"What did you have in mind?"

"I was thinking I could pick you up and take you out to this new place that just opened in Back Bay at Berkeley and Saint James."

"Oh, that's right around the corner from my office."

"Really? Where is your office?" Everything happens for a reason.

"Two Hundred Clarendon. It's that big office building that's all glass."

"I know exactly which building that is." This is going better than I expected. "What time are you off work? I can pick you up and we can walk over to the restaurant."

When we hang up the phone, I’m left with the stupidest shit-eating grin stuck on my face. I actually feel giddy. This girl is going to be trouble for sure.

10

Astrid

Monday mornings just hit different when you're looking forward to a hot date after work. I hate getting up early, especially for work and especially on Mondays. But today, I woke up a full twenty minutes before my alarm went off. I even had time to eat a bagel before leaving my apartment and catching the train.

When Cameron texted me yesterday, I was surprised. I was more surprised that Tyler would give out my phone number to someone he knows I don't know. Of course, I know him a lot more than Tyler realizes, but still.

I'd be lying if I said I hadn't felt butterflies when our eyes met at the Bears game. The same butterflies I felt when I first saw him in Las Vegas. There's no denying our chemistry. I don't have a doubt that we could easily parlay that chemistry into a relationship. But I couldn't keep my fiancé—who I saw and kissed and spent time with every day and would have done anything for if he'd asked—from straying from my bed. How could I keep a professional athlete, who spends half the year travelling and drips sex appeal so hard that women literally throw themselves at his feet, from doing the same? He had hooked up with me on the road, hadn't he? What's stopping him from doing the same in the next city he's in?

Even though Cameron doesn't seem like the type to cheat, neither did Landon at first. Maybe it's foolish of me to even give him a chance, but until I try, I'll never know, right? Cameron would always be this big, mythical sex god that got away. I don't want to live my life with regrets, which is why I agreed to go out with him. Despite my doubts, I am excited for our date.

As much as I wanted to hang out with Cameron yesterday when he'd asked, I follow the old adage: chicks before dicks. Last night was no exception. Bailey had hooked up with a guy from Tinder on Saturday. They went out to a bar to meet up before going back to her apartment. They had sex and then he ended up staying the night. In the morning, he was reluctant to leave, triggering *Operation: Honey I'm Home*.

Operation: Honey I'm Home is a method Bailey and I constructed back in college to get us out of awkward situations, mainly those of the penis-variety. We've been friends for so long that both our apartments have several framed pictures scattered around that show us in various stages of life. There are so many, in fact, that anyone setting foot in either of our apartments for the first time would see pictures of their date with the same woman and assume—correctly—that it's a close friend. The *Honey I'm Home* part plays out when the assumed friend returns home and delivers an Oscar-worthy performance of a scorned lover.

Usually, the clinger leaves without much of a fight. No one wants to be caught in the middle of a fight like that, let alone one that has the woman you thought you just blew away with your love-making abilities screaming at her same-sex partner how bad the sex was and that she didn't even climax. The irony is, with as many times as I've carried out this operation with Bailey, I never expected to be living the real-life version just three months shy of promising "until death."

As I step off the elevator on the thirty-seventh floor, Bailey is waiting for me. She's holding two cups, one of which I'm hoping is my favorite latte.

"I have a cinnamon latte for 'Luckiest Woman on the Planet.'" She holds out one of the cups and we fall into stride together.

With as good a mood as I'm in this morning, I do feel like the luckiest woman on the planet. There's not much that could bring me down at this point...

"Morning, ladies."

Except for that. The sound of Tyler's voice behind us brings Bailey and me to a screeching halt. In all the anticipation of seeing Cam again, I had forgotten about Tyler. I shoot a pleading look over to Bailey, who gives me an awkward grimace before scurrying away to her own office. Traitor.

Spinning on my heel, I take a deep breath and plaster on a smile.

"Tyler!" My voice comes out about an octave too high. I clear the non-existent frog in my throat to give myself some time to come up with something to say. "H-how was the rest of your weekend?"

Not the most eloquent, but all things considered, it could be worse.

Tyler strolls up to me and crosses his arms over his chest. I don't miss the way he tries to make his biceps look bigger. "It was good. I'm glad I caught you. I wanted to talk to you about Saturday."

"Oh, um yeah, okay." Jesus, Astrid, say more than non-words. "Let's go to my office."

I lead him to my office and while I set down my purse and coffee, Tyler clicks the door closed behind him. *Shit.* Here we go.

He clears his throat. "First, I wanted to apologize to you."

My eyebrows shoot up. That's not what I expected at all. "You do?" Here I am feeling like I should apologize to him, not the other way around.

"Yes. I was so nervous about taking you out. I've honestly had a crush on you for a while and when it felt awkward and forced, I thought that alcohol would loosen me up and I just ended up being a jerk. So I'm sorry for getting drunk and abandoning you at the bar."

I blink in surprise. I thought it was just me thinking our date felt awkward. "It's okay, really. The apology isn't necessary."

He nods his head and heaves a big sigh. "Thank you. So, can I make it up to you by taking you out again?"

I draw a deep breath, bracing myself before I speak. "Actually, Tyler, I feel like I should tell you that I have a date with someone else tonight. I know you and I weren't exclusive or anything, but all that to say, I don't think we should see each other again."

He nods, almost looking relieved. Should I be offended?

"So, who's the lucky guy?" he finally asks.

"It's Cameron. We met before, when Bailey and I went to Vegas last summer."

He draws his brows together. "Cameron?"

"Oh, sorry. You'd know him by CJ."

He gapes at me. "Wait, are you telling me you know CJ Grant?"

"Well, I don't really know him. Like I said, our paths randomly crossed in Vegas. I didn't know who he was until Saturday."

"Oh, wow. Well, that's really cool. I'm a huge fan of his." He turns to go before spinning around suddenly again. "Did you get your thing that you left at the bar back?"

"What thing?" I ask, my brows knit together.

"Sorry, back story. Justin McGrady and I exchanged numbers so we could hang out sometime, and he texted me yesterday asking for your number so he could get something back to you that you left at the bar on Saturday." He frowns and gives me a guilty look. "I hope you're not upset by that. I'm sorry, I'm not in the habit of handing out women's phone numbers to random dudes they don't know."

I chuckle. "It's okay, I'm not upset. He passed my number along to Cameron, so it's fine. No one I wouldn't have given my number to myself." I try to suppress my smile. The mere thought of Cam makes me smile.

He laughs and shakes his head. "So that settles it then. Friends?"

I nod. "Friends it is."

"Well, I guess I'll see you around, then." He opens my office door to leave but comes to an abrupt stop. An enormous floral arrangement takes up nearly the entire width of the doorframe.

"Oh Astrid," Bailey's voice calls from somewhere behind the lush greenery. "You've got a not-so-secret admirer."

Tyler raises a brow at me. "CJ?" he asks, tipping his chin toward the flowers.

I can't stop the flush from creeping up my neck, or the huge grin that spreads across my face. No one has sent me flowers before. *Ever*. And these… These are magnificent. They must have cost a fortune.

Bailey carefully guides the arrangement through the doorway and sets the vase on my desk. "Hey, Tyler. Didn't see you there."

Tyler's mouth quirks up in amusement. "I've got to run to a meeting. I'll talk to you guys later."

Bailey gives him an answering smile and a little wave as he leaves. "You guys good? No weirdness?"

I shrug. "We agreed the date was bad and that we were better off as just friends."

Bailey opens her mouth to say something, but the sound of my phone interrupts her. "We'll talk more later," she says, ducking out of my office.

My smile returns as soon as I see who's calling me. I swipe the screen and lift the phone.

"Hi, Cameron."

"Hi, Astrid. Did you get my flowers?" His rich, cozy, masculine voice floats into my ear.

"They're beautiful, thank you." I relax into my desk chair and admire the arrangement again. It's a striking display of white blooms interspersed with deep greenery.

"I'm not sure if you know this," he starts, "but flowers are a language in themselves. Each one represents something and conveys a different meaning."

"Oh, is that right?" This man is full of surprises.

"Absolutely. The calla lilies represent beauty. That's for you, obviously."

"Obviously," I say smiling.

"Mm-hmm." His hum warms me to my core. "Camellias say to the recipient, 'You're adorable,' because you are."

"Okay..." I wait for him to finish.

"The tiny ones are asters, which mainly just reminded me of you because of the name, but they also symbolize love."

The amount of thought that must have gone into this arrangement is touching. "And what about the ferns?"

"Oh, you see, that's my favorite part." He pauses. "The ferns represent magic, for your disappearing act."

I throw my head back, laughing.

"Do you like them?" he asks expectantly.

"I do. They're incredibly thoughtful." I can't believe that I'm tearing up. "Thank you, Cam. It really means a lot."

"I'm glad you like them." He sighs. "I guess I should let you get back to work. I'll see you tonight, beautiful."

"Looking forward to it, handsome." I set down my phone and sit back in my chair, admiring the arrangement again. I smile and let out a small laugh.

In a matter of two days—not even two days—Cameron has firmly planted himself as the most thoughtful person I've ever dated. And technically, we've not even had a date yet.

I feel myself teetering on the edge of a cliff. One that I desperately want to cling to, because I've spent the better part of a year clawing my way back up the rocky ledge after my last fall. I'm afraid if I let myself get too close, I'll fall again and this time, I won't be able to pull myself back up.

11

Cameron

I don't know if I've ever been this excited for a date. When I got off the phone with Astrid earlier, I met up with Justin and a few of the other guys for a morning training session. It did the trick to burn off my nervous energy, but it did nothing to calm the churning in my gut that's telling me tonight has the potential to be a turning point for Astrid and me.

This afternoon dragged on. I found myself watching the clock, wishing it would move faster. I had wanted to snack out of sheer boredom, but there wasn't much in the way of junk food in the house, with it being the day before a string of away games. I tried to distract myself—unsuccessfully—by writing out a grocery list for Jess, my assistant, who would make sure my place was stocked with food by the time I return.

Jess is Justin's little sister. I've known the two of them since we were in elementary school. Jess is six years younger than Justin and me, but she somehow always manages to boss us around. She got a raw deal after nearly completing her biomed degree at Stanford and, in a wild turn of events, ended up getting kicked out in her final semester. Justin convinced her to move out to Boston and stay with him until she got on her feet. While living with him, she took charge of the weekly grocery shopping. From there it turned into her basically running his life, and her career as a professional athlete's personal assistant took off. She's damn good at her job, too.

Looking at the clock again, I finally decide I can't wait any longer and throw on my jacket, planning to walk the short distance from my condo to Astrid's office building just to burn more time until Astrid gets off work. It's a beautiful autumn day, and I use the opportunity to cut through the Public Garden, hoping the tranquility of nature will calm my nerves.

I want to be with Astrid. I want to put in the effort to build a relationship with her. Which is...a new feeling for me. Something about her just draws me in, lights a fire in my chest, and ignites the insatiable need to be close to her. The only thing holding me back from acting on the way I feel about her is her repeated disappearances. I want to be with her, but I need her to want the same. Her continuous sneaking off doesn't scream that she wants to be with me.

Whether it's a lack of trust in the opposite sex from her last relationship or another barrier that she's built up around her heart, there's something holding her back from embracing our connection. I know she feels it the same way I do, her body's physical response alone tells me that. I hope dinner tonight will reassure her that I'm not her asshole ex and I will treat her right.

I make it to the lobby of Astrid's office building a full ten minutes early and rattle off a quick text to let her know I'm here. Pocketing my phone, I stand across the lobby from the elevators, watching the display count down the floors until the doors open and a small crowd pours out. I search the group of people exiting the lobby for Astrid but don't see her. Then another woman catches my attention as she approaches with purpose. She looks familiar, but I can't place her.

"Cameron?" she asks as she closes the distance between us. "You might not remember me, but I'm Astrid's friend, Bailey."

"Hey." I smile as recognition dawns. "It's good to see you again. I hope you're not here to tell me Astrid changed her mind about going out with me."

"Not at all," she laughs. "But I did have something I needed to talk to you about."

"Okay, shoot."

"You know how Astrid's last relationship ended, right?"

My stomach drops, despite her light tone and smiling face. "She shared the highlights, yes."

"Good." All humor in her expression fades. "She's not as tough as she pretends to be. You hurt her, I hurt you. Got it?"

I open my mouth to assure her I wouldn't do anything to hurt Astrid, but the *ding* of the elevator grabs my attention. I look up and am met with a pair of striking green eyes. In a flash, everyone else milling about the lobby ceases to exist. Astrid holds my gaze as she approaches. With every step that brings her closer, more and more of my nerves are calmed, leaving me feeling centered and laser focused.

"You two have fun." Bailey turns on her heel and walks away, touching Astrid's arm as she passes her friend.

Astrid comes to a stop a few feet in front of me. She looks as nervous as I felt just a moment before. I close the distance between us and wrap her in my arms, breathing in her feminine scent and wishing time would stand still.

She pulls back slightly and smiles up at me. "You smell amazing."

I chuckle. "I was just thinking the same thing." I bend and give her a light kiss on the top of her hair. "Let's get going."

We fall into step next to each other, holding hands, walking down the street together like it's the most natural thing in the world. It feels like the most natural thing in the world, too. Being with Astrid feels like a puzzle piece I hadn't realized was missing finally clicking into place.

Stealing a glance at her, I note her appearance. She's more polished than she was on Saturday, wearing her hair straight, light makeup, and a gray business professional dress that clings to her curves and has no reason to be as sexy as it is. I want to slowly peel it off her body and see if she's wearing a matching set of bra and panties.

"So..." Clearing my throat, I try to get my thoughts under control and fight the urge to turn us around, skip the restaurant, and take her back to my condo for a night of intense pleasure instead. Tonight needs to be about getting to know her, not getting her under me. “How long have you lived in Boston?”

She glances over at me, one eyebrow raised as if she can sense where my thoughts had just been. Or maybe, her thoughts were mirroring my own. “Almost five years now. Bailey and I both went to UMass and moved here after graduating.”

“Oh wow. Were you two roommates?”

“For undergrad, we were. Then I met Landon during the first semester of my master’s program, and he had an off-campus apartment I moved into with him. I guess I technically moved here with him.” She takes a deep breath. “But that obviously didn’t work out.”

“I think it worked out just fine.” I grin and give her a wink.

She looks down at her feet and smiles, shaking her head. “Anyway, where did you have in mind to eat?”

“There’s this new Italian restaurant around the corner I thought you might be interested in.”

Her brows knit together in confusion. “New Italian restaurant? There’s only one Italian restaurant around here, and they’ve been booked out for months. There’s no way we’ll be able to get a table.”

“Are you always this negative?” I give her a sidelong look.

She laughs and gives me a quick smack on my bicep that I pretend hurts me, but I’m sure it hurt the back of her hand more.

"Seriously, though. If we can't get a table, there's a burger place up the street a few blocks. It's pretty good too."

"Alright, if we can't get a table at Danza Lento, then we'll go to the burger place. Deal?"

"Sounds good," she says as we round the corner, and the restaurant comes into view.

Danza Lento is tucked into an old brick building, giving the newly remodeled space a rustic and aged ambiance it otherwise would be lacking. The charming atmosphere of the restaurant has no doubt led to its popularity since opening, not to mention the award-winning chef who, by all accounts, puts out nothing but Michelin Star quality food.

The maître d' greets us warmly and leads us to a table toward a secluded area of the restaurant typically reserved for VIPs. There's a bottle of wine waiting for us at the table, as requested, and he makes quick work of opening and pouring us each a glass.

"Thank you, Mario," I say warmly.

"You're very welcome, Mr. Grant. Enjoy your meal." He gives us a parting nod and hurries off.

Astrid raises her eyebrows. "Okay, seriously, how did you get us a table here?"

I shrug. "I may have called in a favor."

"A favor, huh? You know the owner or something?" She lifts her wineglass to her lips.

"Funnily enough, I am the owner," I say nonchalantly.

Her eyebrows soar. "You own Danza Lento?"

"Technically, I'm part owner, and a silent one at that. But yes." I grin mischievously at her.

"Wow, that's..."

"Incredibly sexy?" I finish, hopefully.

She snorts. "I was going to say impressive."

"So, you don't think I'm sexy?"

She smiles over the rim of her wineglass. "I think *you* think you're sexy."

The waiter appears with an appetizer we didn't order and a basket of bread, leaving us just as quickly.

Astrid gives me a puzzled look. "Where are the menus?"

"I asked Maurice to just make us whatever he wanted to." The thought hadn't occurred to me she might be offended by that. "I hope that's okay. I can have them bring over a menu for you if there's something specific you wanted."

"Oh, not at all. That's...that's really nice." She takes a bite of appetizer and closes her eyes. She lets out the sexiest little moan that sends a jolt straight to my cock. "Oh my God. This is delicious."

"You keep making noises like that and I won't be able to make it through dinner." The memory of having her under me and all the little sounds she made come rushing back. My dick remembers too and is now pressing painfully into the zipper of my pants.

She cocks an eyebrow at me and gives me a wicked grin. "This restaurant was your choice. You should have thought about that before bringing me here." She takes a sip of wine.

Since she's clearly in a playful mood, I decide to take a risk. "How do you feel about sex in public places?"

She coughs into her wineglass, sloshing the wine and splashing a bit out onto the white tablecloth.

"I'm so sorry, I was just teasing you. Are you alright?" I lean across the table and touch her elbow, trying to steady her.

She catches her breath and clears her throat before laughing. I wish I could bottle up the sound of it. Hearing her laugh, seeing her smile, I wish I could spend all day, every day with her.

I take a sip of wine and savor it, watching her take another bite. "Okay, serious question."

"Shoot," she says.

"What's your favorite weather and why?"

Her eyebrow quirks up. "Interesting question." She takes another sip of wine while she thinks. "I'd have to say winter. Specifically, right after the first real snow of the season."

I nod. "Interesting answer. Why is that?"

Her eyes fix on a spot behind me, and a faraway look crosses her features. "It's so peaceful. The whole world is calm. All the normal sounds of the city are muffled and absorbed by the snow so that it's just me in a silent corner of the world."

Listening to her get lost in the description makes me realize that this is her, the real her. This is the first time she's let the mask slip and has shown me her true self. I drink it up like water in the desert. The short glimpse of the real her is like a drug, and I'm desperate for my next hit.

I keep asking her questions about herself. She lets the mask slip a few more times, each time giving me another piece of herself, trusting me to hold on to it, if only for a little while.

The rest of our dinner passes all too quickly. It's probably the best meal I've ever had. Maurice really outdid himself. When it's time to leave, I'm dreading saying goodbye.

"Can I give you a ride home? I walked to your office, so I don't have my car, but my condo isn't far from here." I'm hoping that didn't sound too much like a suggestion. I want Astrid in my bed, but only if I know she won't disappear on me again.

"No, that's okay. I'll take the T."

"The T? Is that safe?" I'm not sure what neighborhood she lives in, but I didn't like the idea of her walking alone at night.

Astrid narrows her eyes. "I'm a big girl, I can handle myself."

"At least let me order you an Uber. You've had some wine tonight. I just want to make sure you get home safe."

"First of all, I had two glasses over the course of as many hours. I'm not even buzzed. And second, why do you seem so concerned about my safety?"

I shrug. "I just want to make sure you get home safe."

She frowns at that.

"What?" I ask, suddenly self-conscious and wondering if I've been misreading our time together tonight. "I take care of the things I care about. Let me take care of making sure you get home safe."

She softens to that, blowing out a breath. "Alright. An Uber would be great."

I hand her my phone, and she types in her address before handing it back to me.

"Looks like the driver is about four minutes out." That's four minutes I have to convince her to go out with me again. I take a step closer to her. "I had a really great time with you tonight, Astrid."

She smiles up at me. "I had a really great time with you, too."

I reach up and brush a stray hair out of her face. "I would really like to take you out again."

"I would love that." She's looking at my mouth, and her lips are begging to be kissed. "I'm free Thursday."

I frown. "I'll be out of town. We're leaving early tomorrow morning for an away game. I won't be back until Sunday."

After a single date, this woman has me hating the fact that I have to travel so often. I normally enjoy exploring other cities, even if it is a bit of a whirlwind during the season. *Other cities that aren't in the Midwest, at least.* I struggle to think of exactly where it is we're traveling to this week. *Tampa, followed by Phoenix and Las Vegas. Good.*

Before I can suggest doing something Sunday evening, a black SUV pulls up to the curb and catches Astrid's attention.

"Looks like my ride's here." She doesn't move toward the car, instead she's watching my mouth again.

I abandon the plan-making and opt to give her what we both want. I grab her hips and pull her against me. Her breath hitches as I press the semi I've been sporting all night into her stomach. I bring one of my hands up to cup the back of her neck and pull her in for a kiss. She tastes like heaven, sweet like the tiramisu she had for dessert. Her soft lips part and my tongue dives in, wanting to taste more of her. My cock throbs against her, and she gives me a satisfying whimper and rocks her hips ever so slightly, revealing that she wants me just as much as I want her.

"Hey! You lovebirds order an Uber?" The sound of a man's voice breaks the spell between us, and Astrid pulls back.

We walk over to the curb, and I open the door to the back seat for Astrid. As she climbs in, I lean into the open passenger side window.

"Are you a murderer?" I ask the driver, who blanches instantly.

"Cameron!" Astrid shrieks from the back seat. "He's kidding. I'm so sorry," she says to the driver.

"Get my girl home safe, yeah?" I continue to stare down the driver.

He swallows and gives me a weak nod.

I move to the rear window that Astrid has rolled down. "I'll see you soon." I lean in and give her one last kiss.

"Bye, Cam," she says breathlessly.

I stand there and watch the car pull away from the curb, wondering why it feels like a piece of my heart drove off with it.

12

Astrid

Get my girl home safe. Cameron's words echoed in my head the whole way home and carried me off to sleep on a cloud. That single sentence released a flurry of butterflies in my stomach and was the first thing I remembered as I woke up for work Tuesday morning.

Rolling over in my bed, I reach for my phone on the nightstand and a smile pulls at the corners of my mouth at the sight of a few texts from Cam that he must have sent after I fell asleep.

Cam: Good morning, beautiful. I had a really great time last night. Thanks for not disappearing on me again
Cam: I'll be back early Sunday morning, if you're not doing anything that evening, I'd be thrilled to spend

some more time with you.

The messages release a new flurry of butterflies that carry me through my morning routine and commute to work. The train filled with too many people on their way to work doesn't seem so crowded. The loud traffic on the street doesn't seem so overwhelming.

It's as if I've lived my whole life without realizing the world was tilted and I've constantly been walking up a steep incline, fighting against gravity to reach an unobtainable summit. Now, suddenly, everything has shifted into alignment and I'm no longer fighting the downward pull. I feel a sense of peace, like I've made it home after a long and arduous journey.

There's still an unseen force causing resistance. I may no longer be fighting gravity, but there's still a drag that makes moving forward difficult. I can't quite put my finger on what it is or why it's there, but I feel it holding me back when I so desperately want to move forward. When I was with Landon, I accepted it as my reality. Just a byproduct of being in a relationship and giving part of myself to someone else. With Cameron, it feels like a burden.

I spot Bailey holding two coffees as I step off the elevator onto our office floor. "You must have gotten laid last night."

I shake my head and take the coffee she holds out for me. "No, but damn if I didn't want to."

We make our way farther into the office, greeting our coworkers as we pass.

"So, are you going to tell me what happened?" She looks at me like a kid I just handed a giant present to but told her she had to wait to open it.

"We went to dinner. It was a good time."

Bailey knows how much I hate talking about my personal life in the middle of the office. Especially since rumors of my date with Tyler are still circulating.

"Oh my God, Astrid. Please give me some more details. I'm dying here."

I laugh as I unlock my office door. Now that we're out of earshot of most of the office, I decide to put my friend out of her misery. "You know that new Italian place around the corner that has like a six-month waitlist for reservations?"

"Danza Lento?" She gasps. "Please tell me he used his celebrity status to get you two a table."

"Well, not exactly." I pause to give her a chance to prepare herself. "He's the owner."

Bailey's jaw hits the floor in a very rare stunned-into-silence moment.

"That's what I said," I say, laughing at her shock.

"The owner?" she gapes at me. "Of the restaurant?"

I nod and take a sip of my coffee. "Yeah. He said he's a silent partner, but yes, he is part owner."

"Girl, you are out here living the dream. You've got a sexy as hell pro athlete sending you extravagant floral arrangements and taking you to fancy restaurants he *owns*.

What's next? Buying you expensive jewelry and flying you to an exotic location on his private jet?"

A knock on the door frame has us both turning to look. Tyler is standing there in the doorway with a small teal blue box.

"Morning, ladies." He gives us a small wave. "Astrid, this was just delivered for you."

I take the box from Tyler, and he makes a quick exit. I don't blame him. We may have agreed to be friends, but that was only been twenty-four hours ago. Things are going to be a bit awkward between us for a while.

"You've got to be kidding me. That's from Cameron, isn't it?" Bailey peers over my shoulder.

I pluck the card out from under the white ribbon crisscrossing the top and read it. "'A beautiful, one-of-a-kind necklace for a one-of-a-kind woman. I'll see you soon, beautiful. Cameron.'"

Bailey squeezes my arm as a huge smile breaks out on my face, and a flush blooms in my chest.

I lift the lid and gasp. Sparkling up at me is the most beautiful sapphire pendant necklace on a white gold chain. It's stunning.

Bailey and I gape at each other, neither of us knowing what to say. The sound of my phone buzzing in my purse gets our attention.

I dig through my bag, pull out my phone, and freeze. "It's Cameron."

"Answer it!" Bailey urges.

I quickly swipe to answer the call, hands shaking. "Hello?" My voice trembles. Why am I so nervous?

"Good morning, gorgeous." Cameron's warm voice instantly soothes my anxiety.

"Hi," I say, steeling myself.

"Did you get my gift?" He sounds eager to know if I like it.

I'm not used to getting gifts like this. At least not ones with no strings attached. I'm more accustomed to receiving gifts as a way for people to convince me to do what they want.

My heart sinks. This necklace must have cost more than I make in a month. "I did, and it's gorgeous. But Cameron, I can't accept it."

"What are you doing?" Bailey whisper-shouts at me and tries to grab the phone out of my hand. "Of course you can accept it!"

"I see. And why is that?" Cameron sounds defeated, and I feel like I've just kicked a puppy on Christmas.

I continue to struggle with Bailey, trying to keep hold of both my phone in one hand and the jewelry box in the other. She finally gives up, crossing her arms across her chest and shaking her head disapprovingly.

"It's too expensive," I say to Cameron, feeling defeated myself.

He's silent for a moment before speaking. "Astrid, I'm going to ask you something, and I want you to be honest with me."

"Okay, yeah. What's the question?"

"Do you like the necklace?"

I think I know where this is going. He's going to guilt me into keeping it. I'm not the girl who accepts expensive gifts and sits pretty while a man walks all over me. Not anymore. When I don't respond, Cameron continues.

"Look, Astrid, I got the necklace for you because I wanted you to have it. Nothing more. There are no strings attached here. I wouldn't change a single thing about you because you're already incredible. And I'm not about to take this at a pace that you're uncomfortable with, either. I can see now that this might have been a bit much, but I know after last night that there's no denying you and I have a connection. I feel it and I know you do too.

"We don't have to put any labels on this if you don't want to. Just know that I'm not out here messing around with other people or doing anything that would hurt you. I would never hurt you. I told you last night I take care of the things I care about and that includes you and whatever level of relationship you decide you want and you're ready for."

I fight off the butterflies trying to take flight as I consider his words. He's right, of course. I can feel our connection too. I want to see where this might lead, but this is feeling a little intense for the day after a first date for me. I steal a glance at Bailey. She has her hand clutched to her chest. I don't have the phone on speaker, but I'm sure she heard everything Cameron just said. She mouths, *You can do this.* I close my eyes and take a deep breath as he continues.

"Astrid, I really like you, and I want to be in a relationship with you. I'm not some asshole just out here looking to get you back into bed. I want to see where this goes. Because I think it could be really great."

I smile, unable to hold off the butterflies after a declaration like that. But I also feel like I need to lighten the mood. "Can I ask you something?"

"Yes, of course." His voice is thick with emotion.

"Are you saying you don't want to have sex with me again?"

Cameron's laugh fills my ear. "I would love to have sex with you again, I'd be crazy not to." He pauses and I hear him breathe a sigh of relief. "Say you'll keep the necklace, baby."

Another grin breaks out across my face. "Alright. I'll keep it."

Bailey does a little happy dance over in her corner of my office.

"That's my girl." Cameron's smile comes through the phone. "Listen, I've got to run. Can I see you Sunday? Please tell me you're not doing anything."

I hum, thinking. "I'm free. What did you have in mind?"

"It's a surprise. I'll pick you up at two. Wear something casual and that you can move around in. Don't worry, I'm not planning on fucking you. At least not yet."

I feel my cheeks flush and heat rush to my core, remembering our night in Vegas.

"That works for me," I bite out, trying not to give away how much this man affects me.

"I'll see you Sunday then," he says.

"See you Sunday," I reply.

"Bye, Astrid."

"Bye, Cam." I hang up the phone and look at Bailey again.

She fans herself with her hand. "Jesus Christ you two. Can you turn down the heat?"

I laugh and roll my eyes. "Shut up. Leave me alone, I need to get to work."

"Yes, ma'am," she says as she strolls out of my office.

Then I'm all alone. Just me and the necklace, wondering how in the hell I'm going to make it through the next five days.

13

Cameron

Astrid coming into my life has changed everything. I'm realizing that the reason I never felt like I had time for anyone else in my life was because I never had anyone that I wanted to make time for. And Lord knows, I would give all my time to Astrid.

I wasn't lying when I told her that five days without seeing her was too long. If that seems pathetic and clingy, then fuck it, I'm pathetic and clingy, because every minute I spend away from her feels like an eternity.

The last five days have been a slow and painful torture of practices, away games, press conferences, team meetings, and lots of traveling. Astrid and I have exchanged texts and phone calls when we can. She sent me a selfie on Thursday, and I instantly spotted the necklace I gave her. Damn if I didn't feel proud of myself seeing her wear it.

We won our game against Las Vegas tonight in a shutout. I don't know what's sweeter, beating the reigning Stanley Cup champs at home, being back in the same city that I met Astrid in, or having under twenty-four hours until I get to see her beautiful face again.

Coincidentally, the team is staying at Mandalay Bay, and my room is just down the hall from the room I was in the night I met Astrid. I snap a picture of the room number outside the door and send it to her.

Me: Found my favorite room in Vegas

Astrid: OMG is that THE room??

Me: It sure is. Wonder if the sheets still smell like you…

Astrid: Ew, I hope not.

Astrid: Oh, almost forgot. That was a really nice goal you scored tonight. Good job, handsome

Pride swells in my chest at her recognition, and I can't stop myself from calling her.

She picks up on the first ring. "Hey." Her sleepy voice fills my ear.

"You watched my game?" I blurt out, not caring if I sound pathetic.

"Of course. Bailey came over and we watched it and drank wine. She left a little bit ago and now I'm in bed."

My cock stirs at the thought of Astrid in bed, and I let out a groan. "Fuck, now I'm picturing you naked."

She giggles into the phone. "Well, dang it, Cameron, now I'm doing the same."

"Oh, are you?" I say, readjusting my growing erection. I've never been interested in phone sex, and I don't know if Astrid is into it, but there's not much I wouldn't do to make her feel good. "Maybe we should exchange some pictures so we don't have to imagine it. It has been a good four months since we've seen each other naked."

She hums. "I don't know. I think I should just get some rest. I'm going on a date with a really sexy pro hockey player tomorrow."

I chuckle. "You'll need all the rest you can get for what I've got planned for you." Probably for the best we wrap up this conversation. I'm going to need to give my dick some attention after this.

"I'll see you tomorrow, handsome." Astrid's sleepy voice floats through the phone.

"Looking forward to it, gorgeous." I toss my phone onto the bed and walk into the bathroom.

As I'm turning off the lights in my room, I hear my phone buzz with a text. I'm assuming it's Justin giving me shit for not joining the team in the hotel bar. I unlock my phone and the wind gets knocked out of me.

It's not a text from Justin. It's a picture. From Astrid.

She's standing in front of a mirror in a dimly lit room, turned slightly away from the camera, her hair trailing over her shoulders in messy waves. An oversized knit sweater hangs off one shoulder, exposing the top of a black lace bra underneath. The sweater falls just below her hip, and the way she's standing shows off the plump curve of her ass and her long, toned legs. Her body is even more perfect than I remember and my cock springs to attention. Lord. Have. Mercy.

I wasn't expecting her to send me a sexy picture, but I'm so glad she did. Since she's in a playful mood, I'll have my own fun and send her a picture in return. I turn the lights back on and head for the full-length mirror. I remove my shirt and take in my reflection.

My gray joggers sit low on my hips and they're tight enough that you can easily see the outline of my erection. I snap a picture and check it out before deciding to push my joggers down even lower, exposing the deep cut V of my lower abs, and barely covering the base of my shaft. I snap another picture and send it to Astrid, praying it has the same effect on her that her picture had on me.

I open her picture back up and admire her again. Fuck, it will take every ounce of restraint to keep my hands off Astrid tomorrow. I want to show her how much she drives me wild, how I haven't been able to so much as think about another woman since we first kissed in Vegas months ago. But how am I supposed to do that if she keeps herself closed off? I've got to build up her trust in me first before I give in to the tantalizing attraction I feel for her.

Ever since we met, Astrid has been the one I picture every night, imagining her body curled against mine until I drift off to sleep and she visits me in my dreams. Tonight is no different. Thoughts of her occupy my mind as my sore muscles relax and sleep washes over me.

***

The flight home the next morning is early, but I feel like a kid on Christmas. As soon as my alarm goes off, I'm jumping out of bed, throwing on clothes and rushing down to the buses waiting to take us to the airport.

As soon as we land, I shoot a quick text message to Astrid.

Me: Hi, Beautiful. Just landed. Can I pick you up in about an hour?

Astrid: Hey! That works. You said to dress comfortably, but how comfortable? Like sweats comfy or jeans casual?

Me: Sweats comfy, definitely. Actually, the less you wear, the better
Me: I take that back. We'll be out in public. You definitely need to be covered.
Me: Activewear, if you have it.

Astrid: hmmm... does a thong bikini count as activewear? I feel like I've seen it in Sports Illustrated before...

I nearly trip over someone's suitcase as the image of Astrid's round ass on display pops into my head. God damn, she's not going to make it easy for me to keep my hands off her tonight. For all the innuendos, she may want sex as badly as I do. Despite how much I want to get her in bed again, I want her to feel like she doesn't have to run off before I decide I don't want her anymore, or whatever messed up way of thinking her ex instilled in her that makes her run away.

Me: Astrid, as much as I can't wait to get you naked, it's not the plan for tonight. Text me your address and I'll be over as soon as I've had a long and cold shower.

I pocket my phone before she can respond. If my dick gets any harder, TSA will think I'm trying to smuggle something.

It doesn't take long for me to get back to my condo. I survey the fridge, noting that Jess has been here and stocked up on all my favorites I like to have on hand during the season. I make a mental note to give her a raise and head farther into my condo to the main bedroom.

Twenty minutes later, I'm freshly showered and in my car on the way to Astrid's apartment.

Her place is in Somerville, which isn't super far from where I am in the Park District. I haven't spent a lot of time in that area, but it has a small-town feel to it that seems to fit Astrid well.

I park on the street and make my way up the sidewalk to her door. Her building appears to have seen better days. It must have been built in the 1800s as a duplex and was later divided into more units. Before I can ring the bell, Astrid's door swings open.

She greets me with a wide smile, and I take in the sight of her. Her wavy hair cascades down her shoulders and she's not wearing the heavy makeup like she was last week. She bends to put on sneakers, a little strip of smooth skin peeking out between her high-rise leggings and cropped tee shirt. There's absolutely nothing extraordinary about any one thing she's wearing, but the sum total of it all is sexy as hell.

I can't keep my hands to myself, and I pull her in and wrap my arms around her. I press a kiss to the top of her head and inhale deeply, breathing in the clean scent of her shampoo and the sultry notes of her perfume.

She pulls back to look up at me before speaking. "Hi."

Her glance drifts from my eyes to my mouth and back up again. I cup the back of her neck and press a soft kiss to her lips.

"Hi yourself," I say back. "Are you ready to go?"

"All set." We start back down her sidewalk to my SUV. "So, what have you got planned for us?"

"It's this arcade place for grown-ups. They have bowling, arcade games, a prize counter. It's basically like reliving your childhood." I open the car door for her and help her get settled before jogging around to the driver's side.

"That sounds like a lot of fun. I haven't been bowling in ages."

I pull out onto the street and place my hand on her knee, hoping I'm not crossing any of her boundaries. "You look beautiful, by the way."

Her cheeks flush and she shifts her eyes down to her lap. I give her leg a small squeeze.

"I'm serious. You are," I reassure her, though I don't understand how she can't see it.

She gives me a skeptical look that would have me hauling her across the center console and into my lap so I could show her exactly how beautiful she is if I weren't driving.

Instead, I take a different approach to get her to open up to my compliments. "Did you curl your hair?"

She frowns and glances down at her hair, picking up a lock to inspect it. "Uh, no. These are natural waves. I usually straighten it."

"It looks really good on you. I like it straight too, but the waves are sexy."

She fixes me with another skeptical look.

"What?"

"Nothing. It's just... You're the first guy to ever compliment my hair when it's not straight."

"That can't be true."

She nods.

"But you were engaged." I tighten my hold on the steering wheel. No wonder she wears a mask all the damn time. She's never been with someone who cares enough to let her be herself.

She nods again and heaves a sigh. "Yeah, I was, but he didn't like when I wore my hair wavy. He preferred a more 'polished and sophisticated look on his woman.' Those are his words, not mine. He liked my hair straight, clothing always at least business casual, and a full face of makeup, even if I was just running out to the grocery store."

Rage threatens to bubble up to the surface. "That dude was a fucking idiot. A real man doesn't make a woman ever feel like she has to dress or look a certain way for him." Taking a calming breath, I reach for her hand. "You look beautiful no matter what, but it's when you *feel* the most beautiful that you really shine."

She squeezes my hand and gives me a small smile in return. "Thank you. That really means a lot, Cameron."

I lift her hand up to my lips and plant a soft kiss on her knuckles. I hope tonight goes a long way to erase the expectations her ex placed on her. Astrid deserves nothing less than to be treated like a goddess, and I'll do whatever it takes to be that man for her.

When we park at the arcade, I hop out first and make my way around the car to open Astrid's door for her.

"I can open my own door, you know," she says with a gleam in her eye.

"I know you could, but I'd like to be a gentleman and treat you like a lady."

She leans in close, standing up on her tiptoes to speak into my ear. "And what makes you think I want to be treated like a lady?" She pulls back and gives me a smirk before spinning around and heading toward the building.

"Well, shit," I say under my breath and follow her up to the building, admiring the sexy sway of her ass as she walks away from me. It's a good thing we'll be in a crowded public place. Otherwise, I'd show her just how ungentlemanly I can be, and tonight can't be about that. I need to build up her trust first.

I easily catch up to Astrid before she reaches the doors to the arcade. I hold open the door for her and she giggles as she walks past me and up to the ticket counter.

"Hi there folks," the college-aged kid at the counter greets us. "What can I help you with?"

"Hey, yeah. I think we'd like to get a couple of game cards for the arcade."

"Sure," he says. "Would you like to add on a reservation for a bowling lane or a session of laser tag?"

Astrid and I look at each other.

"Would you like to do either of those?" I ask.

"Can we do both?"

She looks so excited by the prospect that I add on a session of laser tag and a reservation for an hour of bowling.

"And how much were you wanting to load onto the game cards today?" the attendant asks me.

"Let's do two hundred on each," I reply and hand him my card.

We finish up the transaction and head over to the arcade area to scope out our options.

"You didn't have to put that much money on the cards." Astrid says, eyeing the row of Skee-Ball lanes. "I doubt we'll use it all."

I shrug. "If not, then we'll just have to come back. Do you want to get a drink from the bar first or jump right into games?" I glance at my watch. We have about forty-five minutes to kill before our laser tag session.

"I could go for a beer."

We each order a beer at the bar before walking back to the arcade area. I lead Astrid over to the row of Skee-Ball lanes she was eyeing.

"You want to do some Skee-Ball?"

"Always." She takes a drink of her beer. "Let make this interesting, yeah? If I win, you have to take me back to your restaurant."

I laugh, "Deal. But if I win, you'll come over to my condo and let me cook you dinner on Friday."

She gives me a sarcastic gasp. "He cooks too?"

I narrow my gaze at her. "Are you trying to psych me out right now?"

She shrugs. "I don't know why you would think that."

"Baby, I thrive under pressure. You can't rattle me." I smirk.

"We'll see about that," she says as she picks up a ball and launches it squarely into the thousand-point hole.

I blink, totally stupefied.

"When you're done picking your jaw up off the floor, let me know," she says over her shoulder. She picks up another ball and scores another thousand points with ease.

As much as I'd like to say I'm not fazed by her trash talk, I am totally fazed by her trash talk. I was not expecting Astrid to have a strong competitive streak in her. And I am so turned on by it. *Trust first, then sex*, I remind myself.

She whups the living daylights out of me for three straight rounds of Skee-Ball, and I'm grateful she's ready to move on to the next game.

Until she beats me at that one, too. It's fine, basketball isn't my sport. I can let her have the win. She's having a good time and I love seeing her get so excited when she wins.

We move on to a racing game next. She kicks my ass again.

"Cameron Grant, are you letting me win?" She laughs wickedly as she compares the vast difference in our scores.

"Astrid, I'm not letting you win anything. I swear." I can tell she's starting to let go of whatever has been holding her back, and I'm thrilled that winning is helping to accomplish what I wanted. Half of my teammates would be throwing a fit after losing at so many different games but winning isn't everything for me. Gaining Astrid's trust is.

"Do we have time for another race before laser tag?" she asks.

I spy an air hockey table across the arcade. "How about something more in my wheelhouse?" I nod toward it, and she follows my gaze.

"Let's do it!" She bounces out of the simulated racecar seat, and I follow.

"Let's hope you win this one. You've racked up five dinners at your restaurant that you owe me." She gives me a wide, teasing smile.

I start up the air hockey table and drop the puck. Astrid and I exchange the puck a few times, feeling each other out, before she surprises me and launches it into the goal.

She smiles at me and bites her lip. "Oh, come on, don't go easy on me, Cam."

"Wouldn't dream of it, gorgeous." I grin back at her and drop the puck again.

Astrid scores three more unanswered goals on me.

"You know, I think we should maybe head over to laser tag." I push myself away from the air hockey table.

Astrid gives me a wicked grin as she rounds the corner of the table to lean up against the adjacent side. "Oh, I see how it is. You don't want to lose at your own sport."

I laugh. "First of all, my sport is ice hockey. It requires way more skill than air hockey does." I step around the other corner and wrap my arms around her, pulling her in close and speaking softly against the shell of her ear. "Second of all, if you weren't so goddamn sexy when you win, I might actually try to beat you."

She gasps and tries to pull back to smack my chest, but I hold her tight against me so she can't get enough space to bring her arms up.

"I *knew* you were letting me win!"

She continues to struggle to break free from me, but she's laughing at the same time, so I don't let her go. When her movements slow after a few seconds, she looks up at me, chest heaving from exertion. I lean down and plant a kiss firmly on her lips before pulling back to look directly at her.

"The Skee-Ball you honestly did win, though. But once I saw how cute you were when you won, I couldn't help myself."

"Even with this?" She nods to the air hockey table beside us.

"No, you got lucky." I release her and gesture toward the laser tag area. "Let's go crush some kids at laser tag."

Her answering laughter makes my chest swell. I would do anything to hear that sound every damn day for the rest of my life.

14

Astrid

I can't remember the last time I had this much fun on a date. As a matter of fact, I don't know if I've *ever* had this much fun on a date. I feel like I'm a kid again, living completely in the moment. I'm not even mad that Cameron let me win.

We approach the laser tag area, which is already crowded with a couple different groups of college-aged kids. An employee opens the door to the equipment room and we all shuffle in to listen to them explain the rules of behavior.

They explain that the session is set up as capture the flag, so we'll need to split up into two teams, red and blue, and select a captain for each. While we decide which team we should join, one of the kids from the blue team recognizes Cameron and asks if he'll be their team captain. A kid from the red team starts complaining that it's not fair that they should get a professional athlete as it would be an unfair advantage.

"Hold on, guys." One of the other guys from the red team steps forward. "I heard her"— he gestures to me— "talking some serious smack out there at the Skee-Ball lanes. She kicked his ass by like ten thousand points. I say we make her our team captain and let them have Grant."

Cameron gives me a questioning look. "You want to split up to make this a more even match?"

"It won't look so even when we crush you." My voice drips with honey as the boys behind me whoop in excitement.

We all gear up in our sensor vests and the attendant hands both Cam and me a special sensor that will serve as the flag. They go on to explain the rules, which seem simple enough. The game will last for twenty minutes or until one team successfully finds and shoots the other team's flag. If a player's vest gets shot, also deemed a kill, it will cause their laser gun to not fire for a full minute, or until they can return to their home side of the arena and press their gun to a special sensor that will reactivate their equipment. If neither team finds their opponent's flag, the team with the most kills will be the winner. Lastly, they tell us to meet with our teammates to determine a hiding place for our team's flag on our home side of the arena.

I enter the arena and our team huddles up to discuss our strategy. From the way some of these kids are talking about battle plans, they must come here frequently. After a few different ideas are thrown out, we settle on a plan: four players will go on the offensive into the blue team's territory while another group will make it look like they're defending our flag. That's going to be a decoy to draw out and occupy the blue team's offense.

I'll be guarding the real flag from a sniper's nest in a secluded area with only a single path leading to our actual flag. If anyone finds their way up there, I can duck down behind a barrier and avoid getting shot. Anyone who gets close will immediately be killed and either have to wait the full minute before their gun comes back on or go back to the other side of the arena. And, in the event anyone can get past me, they'll still have to find the exact spot where our flag is hidden, which is not in a direct line of sight for anyone except a toddler.

Our plan works flawlessly for the first few minutes of the game. The decoy group draws out the blue team's offense and occupies them entirely, while our offensive group seeks out the blue team's flag.

About halfway through the game, though, the blue team seems to catch on that our defenders aren't actually defending anything. From my vantage point, I can see the blue team branch out and away from the decoy area, drawing out our defenders along with them.

I realize my teammates are going to need some help taking shots. The blue team seems to have more of their players over on our side than we held back to defend our flag. I creep out from my hiding spot to an overlook so I can see more of the arena, but my back is turned to the path that leads up here.

I take out two of the blue team's offense, neither of whom has any idea where the shots came from, and they go running back to their side of the arena to revive themselves. As I take aim at a third blue team member, the sound of footsteps coming up the ramp behind me cuts through the blaring music playing in the arena.

As I'm spinning around in an attempt to shoot whoever found their way up here, my gun slams into a hard male bicep. Before I can create enough distance between us to try to shoot, he grabs my wrists and lifts them over my head. I inhale sharply as his spicy, masculine scent fills my lungs, and he presses his hard body against mine, pinning me against the wall.

Cameron's gaze bores into me, his eyes smoldering with lust. I open my mouth to protest, but it gets lost as Cameron brings his mouth crashing into mine. He doesn't waste any time, and his tongue dives in to meet mine. His kiss is possessive and before I can help it, I'm rocking my hips into him.

He lets out a low growl and shifts his grip on my wrists, freeing one of his hands to roam my body. His touch leaves a searing trail down my arm and side before I feel his fingertips squeeze my hip with a bruising force. He reaches around behind me and grabs onto my ass, changing the angle of my hips so I can feel his hardening cock pressing firmly against my lower abdomen.

I let out a moan and Cameron pulls away from my mouth to trail hot kisses down my jawline. He pulls my earlobe into his mouth and sucks hard. Gasping for air, my arms pull against his grip, and he finally releases my wrists. My hands immediately go to his belt, desperate to get my hands on him.

He lets out a deep chuckle and murmurs into my ear. "Not here, baby. But soon, I can promise you that."

I'm about to protest when the lights on my vest start flashing. The music stops and the lights in the arena come on, making me squint my eyes at the sudden brightness.

"Red team wins!" the attendant announces over the speakers.

My team lets out victory cheers and the blue team starts to grumble.

"You're going to owe me a lot of dinners at your restaurant," I tease Cameron as he takes a step back.

His eyes travel over the length of my body and one corner of his mouth twitches up. "The next time I see you, it'll need to be in the privacy of one of our homes, unless you're an exhibitionist. But I don't think Mario, or the health department, would appreciate me fucking you in the middle of my restaurant."

I fight against the butterflies taking flight in my stomach, not wanting the opportunity to tease him pass me by. I scrunch my nose.

"You think they'd notice?" I cock an eyebrow and grin wickedly at him. "I mean, it's not like it'll last longer than a minute, tops."

I push past him to head toward the arena's exit.

He turns to follow me and plants a nice smack right on my ass. "Maybe for you it won't."

With that, the butterflies take control, releasing a flurry in my core. We both know he's right.

15

Cameron

Oh, God. I'm in trouble. If that kid on Astrid's team hadn't found my team's flag when he did, I wouldn't have been able to tell Astrid no a second time. My only goal when I saw her crouched into an opening and sniping off my teammates was to distract her. But as I crept closer, all the tension that had built up between us earlier fought for release. I shouldn't have taken it as far as I did, not only because we were in an enclosed room with a bunch of young adults, but also because I want Astrid to be sure she wants...whatever this is...before we have sex again. *Trust first,* then *sex,* I reminded myself for the millionth time today.

Watching Astrid cut loose has been a blast. When we were at the restaurant last week, I caught glimpses behind the mask she puts on for others, but today, that mask has almost completely fallen away. If I can get that last little bit to vanish, if she can trust me enough to allow me all the way in, I could die tomorrow and feel like my life was complete.

We make our way over to the bowling lanes, grab some shoes, and spend a few minutes picking out balls. Astrid gets our names entered into the screen while I go grab us a pitcher of beer from the bar and place an order for a pizza to be delivered to our lane.

I laugh when I notice the names she entered while I was gone. "Ass-trid and BJ 4 CJ?"

She giggles, "I thought it was only appropriate, given that you haven't missed a single opportunity to stare at my ass all day long."

I pour two glasses of beer for us and hand her one. "So, it's safe to say that you've been thinking about blowing me all day, then?"

She shrugs and walks up to the ball return, grabbing a sparkly pink ball, but for all her bravado, I don't miss the way her cheeks flushed right before she turned away from me. I watch as she lines up to throw her first frame, and I can't help but check out her ass. Damn. She might have been right about the name.

Astrid launches the ball, and it goes flying down the lane, arcing so close to the gutter that I think it's going to fall in before veering back toward the center and sending the pins flying in every direction.

"Oh shit," I say as she turns around and starts walking back toward our table.

"I know, that was sloppy. It's been a while." She flops back into her seat.

My face contorts in confusion. "Astrid, that was a perfect strike."

She shakes her head. "That was far from perfect. Did you see where the ball hit? I was way too light on the pocket."

I blink at her. "You're an actual bowler?" I can't believe she's about to hustle me out of another win.

"Well, no. Unless you count bowling in high school and college to be an actual bowler."

I laugh, "You're amazing, you know that?"

She shrugs. "I'm alright. I've never hit a perfect game or anything close."

I pin her with a look. "Astrid, I'm not talking about bowling."

A flush spreads across her cheeks with a matching smile on her lips, and fuck if it doesn't take my breath away. I love knowing how easily I can affect her.

"It's your turn." She nudges my arm, and I push up from the table to throw my own first frame.

I'm rusty but manage to put up my own strike. I walk back to the table and plop down, feeling Astrid's eyes on me the whole time. Picking up my beer, I meet her eyes over the rim of my pint glass and take a drink.

"How often do you wax your balls?" She cocks an eyebrow.

She times her question perfectly, waiting for the moment the beer hits my open mouth, causing me to cough into the cup and slosh beer down my chin.

She laughs manically and hands me some napkins, clearly enjoying seeing me flustered. I can't be mad, though; the sound of her laughter makes my chest swell. If it weren't for the cold beer that dripped down to my crotch, that would be swelling too.

"I'm going to get you for that," I say, laughing.

Her eyes gleam with mischief. "We'll see." She stands to go play her next frame.

This time, her first ball leaves a few pins. She easily picks them off in a spare. As long as she doesn't keep throwing strikes, I might have some hope of winning here.

By the end of our second game of bowling, I've managed to squeeze out more pins than Astrid, mostly due to the fact that she left a pin standing in the tenth frame, missing out on her chance at a third roll, and I put up a turkey, three strikes in a row.

"Well, since this is the only game you *didn't* let me win, I suppose our earlier wager applies. Congratulations on your victory, Cameron. I will happily accept you cooking me dinner as the cost of my loss." She looks over her shoulder at me as she changes back into her shoes.

She stands and I pull her into my arms. "I could make good on that tonight if you'd like."

Astrid gives me a questioning look. "But we already ate pizza."

"I can think of a few ways to work up an appetite." I bend down to press a soft kiss to her lips.

She sighs. "As much as I would love to, I can't tonight. I might have to help Bailey with something later."

"That sounds like an excuse," I say, bending further to kiss her neck and she rolls her head to the side to give me more access. "Are you sure I can't change your mind?"

She takes a deep breath and presses her palms against my chest. That's my answer then. I pull back and look down at her.

"What about Friday? Come over after work. I don't have a game until late Saturday, and we don't leave for our next away game until next Sunday."

She smiles up at me. "That sounds great."

"What do you say we go over to the prize counter to see how many tickets you racked up beating the crap out of me in the arcade?"

She laughs, "Lead the way, handsome."

16

Astrid

"It looks like you've got four hundred and fifty thousand tickets available. Do you want to redeem all of them tonight?"

Cameron and I both stare at the prize counter clerk.

"Sorry, did you say four hundred and fifty?" I scan the shelves and take in all the little trinkets and stuffed animals, all redeemable for anywhere from one to five hundred tickets.

"No, ma'am. Four hundred and fifty *thousand,*" the clerk clarifies.

"Damn, Astrid. I told you that you kicked my ass." Cam nudges me with his elbow.

"That's a *ton* of prizes," I say, still taking in all the options. From the looks of it, I can get one of everything and still have some tickets left over.

Cam points to a teddy bear close to six feet tall hanging up in a corner that I hadn't noticed. Talk about not seeing the forest for the trees.

"She'll take that," he says to the clerk before turning to me and winking. "For when I'm on the road."

Sweet Jesus. I'm pretty sure I just melted into a big puddle on the floor.

We finish redeeming all the tickets for as many prizes as we can and exit the arcade, laughing at how hard we're struggling to carry everything.

"Please don't be offended, but I'm going to need to set this stuff in the back before I open your door for you," Cam says as we approach his SUV.

I laugh, "I'll give you a pass this time."

Cam opens the rear hatch and throws the things he's carrying inside before turning and doing the same with the things I'm carrying. We round the SUV, he opens the passenger door for me, and I climb in.

A second later, Cam opens the rear driver's side door and puts the giant teddy bear into the seat. He even buckles it in before slamming the car door closed. I'm laughing as he gets behind the wheel.

As we drive away from the arcade, I scroll through Cameron's Spotify and pick some music for us to listen to. I find a classic rock playlist and hit shuffle.

The first song comes on and Cam starts drumming his fingers on the steering wheel and singing along. He looks over at me and holds out his hand, and I take it. He traces the line of my index finger with his thumb as he continues to drum on the steering wheel with his other hand. I sigh contentedly, realizing how completely normal this all feels.

"What's that smile for, gorgeous?" Cameron's soft voice drifts into my thoughts.

"I was just thinking about how much I enjoyed all of this. I don't think I've ever had this much fun on a date."

He glances over at me with a surprised look. "I don't know if I believe that."

My eyes drop to my lap, and I watch his thumb as he continues to trace circles on my hand. I'm not proud of this part of my past.

"It's true. Besides a few casual dates I had in high school and college, Landon was my only serious boyfriend. Our dates were never about having fun with each other. It was always about putting on a show. For his coworkers, his parents, for anyone who happened to be looking. I spent years trying to fit into the mold of what he thought a girlfriend and wife should be, you know?" I glance over at him and see his jaw tick. "Anyway, I had forgotten how much fun it was to just be myself." I try to smile, but it wavers on my face.

Cam squeezes my hand. "I'm so sorry you went through that. You deserve someone who sees how amazing you are. The real you, that is. Not some version of you that others expect you to be."

I nod in agreement. "Well, hindsight is twenty-twenty. I know what I deserve now, and I won't settle for anything less."

He looks over at me and flashes a smile. "That's my girl."

I smile right back. "I'm your girl now, am I?"

I'm trying not to get in my head about this moving too fast. We've only gone on two dates, but this feels right.

Being with Cameron feels like home. And hearing him call me his girl? I'd crawl into his lap right now and hump his brains out if he weren't busy navigating through Boston traffic.

He squeezes my hand. "Damn straight you are. Oh, and by the way, I give you full permission to kick me squarely and directly in the nuts if I ever make you feel like you need to be anything but one hundred percent yourself."

I snort out a laugh. "That's the most romantic thing I've ever heard."

He laughs in return. "Your ex really set the bar low for me, didn't he?" He inhales deeply and licks his lips. "I like this side of you. A lot, actually."

"Oh? And what side is that?"

He pulls up to the curb in front of my apartment and puts the car in park before turning to face me.

"The real one."

He looks at me with such intensity that all the air feels like it just got sucked out of the car. He reaches up and cups the side of my face, his thumb tracing along my cheekbone.

"I'm serious about what I said. You deserve to be with someone who sees and appreciates you for who you are."

Maybe it's the adrenaline still coursing through my veins from our time at the arcade or maybe it's the butterflies taking flight in my stomach, but for a moment, my brain takes a backseat.

"Are you saying you want to be that person?"

He smirks. "I've already said you're my girl, so I think you know the answer to that question. I think the more important thing for you to ask is whether or not *you* want me to be that person."

I lean into his touch, considering what I want.

He smiles at me and glances at the back seat. "Come on, let's get all this stuff inside."

I run ahead to unlock the door that leads to the flight of stairs up to the second floor. Cameron has somehow managed to carry everything in one trip. I can barely see him past the giant teddy bear and various trinkets all wrapped in his strong arms. He's walking like he's trying to carry a thousand pounds and the sight of his overexaggerated movements brings a laugh bubbling up from my throat.

"Hey, don't laugh." He grunts, peeking out from behind the enormous teddy bear. "This is exactly how we met."

The memory of being loaded down with takeout bags and rushing to catch the elevator at Mandalay Bay brings another wave of laughter out of me as I follow Cameron up the stairs.

"You can throw everything on the couch." I motion at the living area of my studio apartment.

He drops the prizes on the couch, carefully placing the teddy bear in a seated position before turning back toward me.

"So," he says, surveying our surroundings, "this is the place, huh?"

I look around, suddenly self-conscious of my humble apartment. I know Cameron won't judge me for having such a small place, but he's only standing about ten feet from the bedroom area.

"This is it." I shrug. "It's not much but it's really the only living space I've ever had all to myself."

He motions toward my bed. "I like your..." He clears his throat. "All your pillows."

I snicker. "No you don't."

"You're right. You caught me looking at your bed and I had to come up with something."

He opens his arms and I step into his embrace. "What are you doing tomorrow?" he asks, pressing a kiss to my hair.

"Working. Pitching a new campaign to a client. What are you doing tomorrow?"

He squeezes me tighter. "I meant after work. I have a seven o'clock game. I was wondering if you might want to come watch."

I look up at him and smile. "I'd really like that."

He beams at me. "Yeah? I'll send over two tickets to your office in the morning so you can bring someone along."

I give him an innocent smile. "That's so nice of you. There's this guy at my office who's a huge hockey fan. He'll be so excited."

Cam narrows his eyes at me and squeezes his arms tighter around me. "You can bring anyone *except* Tyler."

I raise my eyebrows at him. "Oh, jealous, are we?" It's a damn good look for him, that's for sure. "You can relax, I'll bring Bailey. She knows nothing about hockey, but she loves athletes."

He brings his mouth to mine and traces a soft kiss over my lips. I tangle my fingers into the hair on the back of his head and he inhales sharply, prodding the seam of my lips with his tongue. I welcome him in, swirling my tongue with his, our bodies desperate to devour each other. Then he breaks our kiss, resting his forehead against mine and brushing his thumbs over my cheekbones.

"I better get going. If I don't go now, I'll throw you down on that bed and fuck you so hard, your neighbors will call the cops."

I swat his chest, mocking offense. "I am not that loud in bed."

A low laugh caresses me as he trails hot kisses down my jaw until his breath tickles my ear.

"Yes, you are." He continues to kiss down my neck to my collarbone. "Nothing to be ashamed of, gorgeous. It's a huge fucking turn on."

A rush of heat zips down my spine and settles right in my core. I press my hips into his, trying to convince him to continue our kiss with my body.

He laughs again and releases me. I don't miss how he has to readjust the front of his pants when he steps back.

I walk with Cam down the stairs to the landing and my front door. We say goodbye and I stand there in the open doorway, watching him walk down the sidewalk to his car.

"Cameron," I call after him.

He spins around, eyebrows raised in question.

I take a deep breath and speak before I lose my nerve. "I want you to be that person."

An enormous smile spreads across his face.

"It's about time you figured that out." With a wink, he turns and continues down the path to his SUV. Before he gets in, he pauses and looks at me over the front hood. "See you tomorrow, gorgeous."

He gets in his car and drives off, leaving me alone with the butterflies that carry me back upstairs.

***

The next morning at work, Bailey pops into my office with two coffees as soon as I sit in my chair.

"You must have had a horrible time last night if you beat me here on a Monday morning," she jokes and slides a cup that looks like my favorite latte across the desk, then sits opposite me.

I can't help but smile. Yesterday was amazing. "I've never had that much fun on a date before."

She raises her eyebrows and peers at me over the rim of her cup. "Vegas included?"

I scrunch my brows together, confused. "We didn't have sex."

"You didn't?" she says, a bit too loud.

I glance toward my open office door and hold my hand up in a shushing gesture to her.

"I really wish I would have known that. I needed you to come over for Operation: Honey I'm Home, but I didn't want to interrupt!"

"Ooof," I say. "Was it that bad?"

Bailey had asked if I would be available, if needed, to kick out a Tinder date from her apartment. That had been the reason for not going back to Cameron's place after the arcade. When I hadn't heard anything from her, I assumed the date had either gone well or the guy had left without issue, if not both.

She glares at me. "It was worse than the time there was an actual gas leak and the guy still refused to leave."

I laugh, "Oh hey, I forgot about that guy."

The firemen had to physically remove him from the building. Bailey must have some magic lady parts for all the guys that like to hang around when she's done with them.

"Me too, honestly." She gets a misty look on her face. "He was really good with his tongue. And he had a big nose."

I make a face. "I don't want to know."

She's now totally glazed over. "I wonder what he's been up to lately... I might text him later."

"Actually," I say, trying to snap her out of her horny trance. "We have plans for tonight."

She gasps, "What are we doing tonight?"

As if on cue, Tyler appears in the doorway with a huge gift box, looking annoyed as hell.

"Okay seriously, we have a team of thirty-four interns. Why are you the one running deliveries for them?" Bailey says to him.

"They're all in the conference room trying to come up with a new TikTok dance for a sports drink company," he says dejectedly.

"Thanks for dropping this off, Tyler," I say genuinely.

He gives a curt nod and walks out of my office.

"Is he okay?" I ask Bailey. Tyler is usually the office sunbeam.

"No idea." Bailey tips her chin toward the box. "What's that?"

"It's supposed to be our tickets to the Bears game tonight, but this is definitely way more than a ticket."

The sound of my phone ringing draws our attention away from the box.

"That man's timing is impeccable." Bailey laughs.

I pick up my phone and, sure enough, Cam's name lights up the screen.

"Hello?" I answer.

"Good morning, beautiful." Cam's warm, smooth voice instantly brings a smile to my face. "Did you get my gift?"

"That depends. Did you send me the world's biggest hockey ticket?"

He laughs. "So, you haven't opened it? Go ahead, I want to hear your reaction."

He sounds excited and that, combined with his history of giving expensive gifts, makes me very nervous. Removing the navy and gold bow that crisscrosses the package, I lift the lid and remove the tissue paper. Inside the box are two Boston Bears jerseys. One with Cameron's last name spelled across the back, the other with a name I don't recognize.

"Who's 'Charbonneau?'" I ask.

"That's Reid. It's his first year in the NHL and his jersey sales have been slow. I thought Bailey might need something to wear. Two birds, you know?"

I hand Bailey her jersey and hold up the one with "Grant" spelled across the back. "This is really thoughtful. Thank you, Cam."

"Yes, thank you, Cameron!" Bailey shouts from across my desk.

I switch my phone to speaker, and the sound of Cam's laughter fills my office.

"You're welcome. There should be an envelope in the box too with your tickets. As well as some vouchers for food and drinks."

I root around in the box for the envelope and open it.

"Cameron," I say, fanning out the contents. "There's like three hundred dollars' worth of vouchers in here. Are you sure we'll need that much?"

He laughs again. "Maybe not, but I want you to have a good time and not have to worry about the pricing. They don't expire until the end of the season, so if you don't use them all, you can keep them for next time."

"Thank you again. This is amazing." I smile, feeling the blush wash over my cheeks.

"No problem, I'm excited for you to come. I'll let you two get back to work, though. I've got to run to practice, anyway."

"Okay. See you tonight," I say.

"Astrid, take me off of speaker for a second."

I frown at the phone, wondering where this is going. I hit the speaker button and hold the phone back up to my ear.

"Am I off speaker phone now?"

"Yes," I say hesitantly.

"Good. Because I wanted to tell you that when you come over on Friday, I want you to bring that jersey and wear it while I bend you over the arm of my couch and fuck you from behind."

I look up at Bailey, who clearly was able to hear that whole... thing... because her jaw is on the floor. I'm sure the expression on my face matches hers.

"Anyway, beautiful," he continues, "I'll see you at the game." And he ends the call.

I set the phone down and look at the jersey again, heat spreading to my core at the image Cameron conjured up.

"Damn girl!" Bailey gasps, fanning herself with one hand.

I look up at her and she's blushing. So, it's not just my hormones reacting to him, then. That makes me feel a little better.

***

Bailey and I walk into a crowded TD Garden that is buzzing with excitement. Music blares over the speakers, and the Jumbotron shows groups of fans who jump with enthusiastic waves and dance for the five seconds before the camera lands on another group.

"Holy fuck," Bailey exclaims when we finally find our seats. "This is so close!"

Our seats are situated against the glass between the home and away team benches.

The lights turn off and cheers from the crowd erupt, catching both Bailey and me off guard.

The arena buzzes with electricity as the Bears take the ice for their warm-up. They speed past us in circles with such intensity that I'm not sure how they don't collide with one another.

Suddenly, one of the players stops directly in front of us and holds up a gloved hand to the glass for a high-five. It takes me a moment to recognize the behemoth grinning down at me. The skates and equipment make Cameron seem twice his normal size. He winks at me from his side of glass and skates away to start their shooting drills.

Two other players stop directly in front of us and hold their gloves up to the glass to give us high fives. One of them I recognize as Cam's friend, Justin. The other I don't recognize until they skate away, and I see the name on the back of his jersey is the same as on Bailey's jersey.

"Oh Astrid, I think I may love hockey." Bailey's eyes are locked on a group of players doing some overtly sexual hip and groin stretches.

I laugh, "I knew you'd enjoy this."

After all the pre-game announcements and national anthem, the starting lineups take the ice. Cameron skates to center ice to face off with the center from the away team. The two look poised to physically fight each other, the aggression sending a shiver down my spine.

As soon as the puck drops, Cam zips down the ice with the puck faster than my eyes can track. The players all skate so fast that it's hard to keep track of who has the puck. Cam and Justin make a play on the goal that the goalie blocks easily, and a forward from the other team zooms past us with the puck in a breakaway.

Just as he's lining up to shoot on our goalie, Reid appears out of nowhere and checks him hard into the boards. Justin is there to grab the puck back, and he and

Cam zoom back to the other end of the arena. Before I know what's happening, the lamp on top of the goal lights up and the crowd erupts in cheers. Bailey and I jump to our feet, swept up in the excitement of it all.

As the crowd settles down, Justin and another player from the opposing team get in each other's faces. The crowd stirs back to life, chanting for a fight. Tension between Justin and his opponent only intensifies, until suddenly, both players toss their gloves to the ice and start throwing punches.

Bailey sucks in a breath and grabs my arm. We watch the two brawl for what seems like forever. It takes three referees and a couple players from each team to separate them, and each is escorted to their respective penalty box.

The rest of the first period passes quickly and with such intensity that it has me feeling exhausted from just watching. I catch Cameron's eye as he leaves the ice with his team, and he gives me a wink. Cue butterflies.

"Girl, you've got that drooly look on your face again." Bailey's teasing voice drifts into my thoughts.

I roll my eyes. "Don't act like you haven't been drooling over Charbonneau all night."

"Ew, no," she says, scrunching up her face. "That kid looks like he just turned eighteen."

"Ahh, I see. So, it's Justin you've been drooling over all night, then?" I wag my eyebrows at her.

And then, something happens that almost never happens with Bailey. She blushes for the second time in a single day.

"Oh my God!" I exclaim. "You *like* Justin!"

"I do not," she says way too quickly.

"Liar."

Now it's her turn to roll her eyes. "I can appreciate the beauty and athleticism of a finely tuned male body without wanting to fuck it."

My voice goes up an octave, and I raise my eyebrows in doubt. "I never said anything about sex. That must mean you *definitely* want to fuck him."

She huffs out a sigh. "Well, can you blame me? The man is built like a freaking Greek god."

I laugh, "Cam says he's a big-time player, so he'd probably take you up on the offer if you asked."

She fixes me with a look. "I'm not *that* desperate."

I decide to let her off the hook, at least for now. "What do you say we try to burn through some of these concession vouchers?"

"Yes, please. If I'm going to sit here and watch these hockey players drip with sex for two more periods, I'm going to need some beer to calm me down."

I hook my arm in hers and we make our way through the arena, back to the concession stand.

17

Cameron

"Let's keep up our momentum. Remember what we've been drilling this week. Don't lose focus!"

Coach's words cut through my thoughts about Astrid, proving the need for his reminder.

"Yes, Coach!" The whole team answers him in unison.

He goes on to lay out the plan for the second period, highlighting a couple of plays we've been honing while on the road over the last couple of weeks. We squeezed it out last week in Tampa, barely. It was messy but we managed. Even with the minimal number of fans in the stands, the crowd went feral. If we can pull it off at home, they might literally start a riot.

We rush down the chute and onto the ice, ready to pull off the most complicated play in our playbook.

I try my best to stay focused on the game, but I feel her eyes on me. I look over in her direction, my eyes homing in on her slender body clad in my jersey, and I have to stifle a moan. Just seeing her with my name sprawled across her back has my cock perked up, ready to play his own stick game.

I blow out a breath as I take position at center ice, ready for the first faceoff of the second period. It's time for the crowd to lose their fucking minds.

I win the face off easily. Chicago's center is slow as fuck, despite being a whole five years younger than me. I clip the puck over to Justin. He skates along the boards toward their defensive zone and one of their players takes the bait. Perfect.

Justin fakes losing the puck flawlessly when their defender checks him into the boards, losing his tail when he uses their momentum against them. He easily picks the puck back up and passes it to me.

I go one-on-one with their other defender. As soon as he makes a move to swipe the puck back over to his buddy, who's still on the boards with Justin, I give the puck a love tap in the opposite direction. It gives me enough space from the defender to push into no-man's-land.

From the corner of my eye, I see Reid skating to the corner to set up the next part of the play. I tip the puck right into his stick as he goes behind the net, with the defender who was just covering me going to meet him. The defender and goalie both expect him to come out the other side and try to slip the puck in the two-hole. But Reid is a maniac with a stick and instead, flips the puck around, keeping it almost invisible to everyone except those of us who know where to look. The goalie leaves almost half of the net open, and before either he or any of his teammates realize where the puck is, I send it flying in between the posts. It's a fucking thing of beauty.

The resulting cheer from the crowd is deafening. My teammates rush me to celebrate, but my focus is now on Astrid. I lock eyes with her and point directly at her, telling her that one was all for her.

***

After our shut out at home on Monday, we played back-to-back away games on Wednesday and Thursday. It's not often that we have three wins in a row and as sweet as victory is, it's nothing compared to the prospect of spending the night with Astrid.

I'm a little embarrassed to realize that I'm nervous about having her over tonight. I've built up this night with her so much in my head that I'm hoping I can live up to my own expectations. I even had my housekeeper come and do a deep clean while I was on the road this week to have everything perfect.

I check the neat piles of hand-rolled pasta drying on the counter and put a pot of water onto the stove to boil. As I'm tasting the Bolognese for the hundredth time, trying to occupy myself, a knock announces her arrival.

A huge stupid grin breaks out on my face as I round the massive kitchen island. I swing open the front door and take in the sight of her. We lock eyes and I feel like I just got body slammed into the boards by a 250-pound goon at full speed.

"Hey," she says uneasily. At least I'm not the only nervous one.

"Get in here, gorgeous." I haul her into my arms, burying my face in her wavy hair, and breathing in her clean, feminine scent. "It's good to see you."

She pulls back to look up at me, grinning. "That was a hell of a game last night."

Fuck, this woman is perfect. I lift her chin higher and give her a soft kiss, which quickly turns into tongue-fucking her mouth like my life depends on it. There's something about Astrid I find irresistible. I release her and take a step back because if I don't put some space between us, I'll haul her sexy ass straight to my bed.

"Come on in. I'll give you the grand tour." I take her coat and lead her past the kitchen and into the living room.

She scans the living room furnishings, eyes wide like a kid on Christmas. "This place is amazing," she says. "It must cost you a fortune."

"Nah, it wasn't too bad." Self-conscious, I put my hands in my front pockets.

"Oh, is that right? I didn't realize penthouses were that affordable." She gives me a teasing grin. She's got me there.

I watch as she moves closer to the floor to ceiling windows that overlook the Public Garden. A dream-like look washes over her features, beckoning me to edge closer to her.

"Wow." She breathes out the word, taking in the view.

I come up behind her and wrap my arms around her, pulling her back against me. I lean down to speak softly into her ear. "That's the—"

"Public Garden," she cuts me off. "I know. It's my favorite place in the city. I've never seen it from above, though."

I brush her hair over to her opposite shoulder, exposing the elegant column of her neck. "It's one of my favorite places, too." I say against the shell of her ear. "Do you get over there very often?"

She sighs. "Not as often as I'd like. At least not anymore." Sadness tinges her voice and I'll be damned if I let this woman be sad in my arms.

"Maybe we can go for a walk over there in the morning." I trail gentle kisses down her neck.

"I'm staying the night now, am I?"

"You tell me," I murmur against her supple skin. "You're stunning."

She whimpers and tilts her head further to the side, allowing me more access. *Fuck*. I've got to at least make it through dinner before letting my dick make any more decisions for me.

Then the loudest growl bubbles up from Astrid's stomach and she stiffens, frozen in my arms.

I nuzzle back into her neck, trying not to let the moment go just yet. "Are you hungry, beautiful?"

She laughs, "I'm starving. I skipped lunch."

"Come on. Dinner's almost ready." I lead her back into the kitchen, pour two glasses of wine, and pass her one. I add salt to the boiling water on the stove and toss in the little bundles of pasta.

"So," I say over my shoulder, "what happened that made you skip lunch?"

She takes a sip of wine, and I watch the long column of her throat move as she swallows. "Just a client thing. You know, one of those 'everything is an emergency' types. By the way, that smells amazing. What are we having?"

I smile and give the sauce a stir. "Homemade pappardelle with Bolognese."

I grab a spoonful of sauce and walk over to where she's sitting on the other side of the island. I hold the spoon up to my mouth and blow on it, so it doesn't burn her mouth before holding it out to her to try.

She wraps her lips around the spoon and her eyes flutter closed on a moan. My cock jerks at the sight. It's going to be harder to get through dinner than I thought.

18

Astrid

I open my eyes as Cam takes the spoon out of my mouth. He's looking at me like an animal watching their prey. The heat of his gaze sends a shiver down my spine and my core throbs, remembering the last time I saw that look in his eyes at the arcade.

My voracious stomach ruins the moment once again, demanding more food. The real reason I didn't eat lunch was because I was so nervous. I would never let a client get in the way of food. I've had butterflies in my stomach all week in anticipation of tonight.

He snickers and heads back toward the stove. "It'll be ready soon, don't worry."

Right. Worry is all I've done. What if the sex isn't as great as I remember? What if the allure of meeting a mysterious stranger in a hotel accounted for the majority of the chemistry we had in Vegas?

I push my self-doubt away, telling myself that can't be the case. We've gotten to know each other on a deeper level now and I still feel electricity pop and spark whenever he gets close. But that's over the last, what, two weeks now? Shit. The doubt creeps back in. How well can we actually know each other?

"Can I use your bathroom?" I ask. Maybe a little space will help me settle down.

"Sure, it's just down that way." He motions back the other way down the entrance hall, away from the living room and kitchen.

I wander down the hall, admiring again the cleanliness and neatness of Cam's condo. The small washroom has minimal décor, except for an old, framed photo. It shows what looks like maybe a ten-year-old boy, beaming at the camera while an older man leans over the open hood of an old car. The older man looks at the boy with a twinkle in his eye. I get the sense that the boy is Cameron, but I'm not sure who the older man is. He must be his grandfather, the one who he was so close with.

I join Cameron in the kitchen again, my stomach still in a tight knot. I watch him from the other side of the island. His strong forearms flex as he transfers pasta from the boiling water into the saucepan. The fabric of his dress shirt stretches tight over his muscular shoulders and back.

I'm drawn to him like a moth to a flame. I move almost as if I'm possessed, not fully in control of my own body. Without him noticing how close I am, I place my hands on his shoulder blades and smooth them down the tightly coiled muscles of his back before trailing them around his waist and wrapping my arms around him. I press my cheek into his back, taking in the clean, masculine scent of him.

He looks at me over his shoulder and brings one of his arms up and over my head as he turns around.

"Hey, you." He wraps me in his arms and kisses the top of my head. "You ready to eat?"

"Mm-hmm." I look in the pans on the stove. "It smells so good. I'm starving."

He nods toward the dining table. "You take a seat. I'll grab everything for us."

I sit at the already set table and watch Cameron move swiftly around the kitchen. He grabs a bowl of salad out of the fridge and two small plates out of a cabinet and sets them on the table. A moment later, he sets a plate filled with the delicious-looking pasta in front of me. He refills our wine glasses and finally sits.

He holds up his glass to toast. "To the chance encounters and twists of fate that led us here. And to your incredible skills as a magician that I hope you won't use on me again."

I tip my head back in laughter. This man has cemented himself so firmly into my life that I can't imagine disappearing on him again. I smile back at him and clink my glass to his. "Cheers."

We eye each other over the rims of our glasses and drink.

Unable to wait any longer, I dive into the plate of pasta sitting in front of me. I close my eyes and let out a moan. "Oh my God, this is so good."

"Thank you, I'm glad you like it." He eyes me, and I catch the corner of his mouth twist up in a smirk before he grabs his wine glass and takes a drink.

"What?" I ask, suddenly self-conscious.

He shakes his head. "Nothing, just thinking about all the little things that had to fall into place for us to meet, and then to find our way back to each other."

I smile back, giving up my efforts to calm the butterflies and just let them explode in my stomach instead. "It is pretty crazy, isn't it?"

We continue to eat and talk about all the little moments that had to align for our paths to cross. If Landon hadn't cheated. If I hadn't upended my whole life months before our wedding, refusing to stand by him after he played me for a fool or accept him having a mistress as an inevitability of high society. If Bailey hadn't dreamed up a girls' weekend in Vegas to get my mind off things. If the Bears hadn't won their division in the playoffs. If Tyler hadn't dragged me to a hockey game in what turned out to be the worst first date and consequently best bar meet-up I've ever had. If Justin hadn't been so sneaky and convinced Tyler to give him my phone number.

At any one of those moments, the train bringing us together could have derailed and Cameron and I would have either never met or would have never found each other again. Sure, you could argue that Boston isn't that huge and, given the proximity of my workplace and his condo, we may have bumped into each other eventually. But I'm starting to buy into Cam's belief that everything happens for a reason.

I push back from my plate and toss my napkin on the table. "I'm stuffed."

"Me too." Cameron wipes his mouth. He pushes back from the table and approaches my chair, extending a hand to help me to my feet.

I stand and look up at him, expecting him to turn toward the dishes and start clearing. Instead, he reaches up and tucks a strand of hair behind my ear, trailing his fingertips down the side of my throat to my collarbone.

"You wore the necklace I gave you." His voice is deep and gravelly.

He dips his head closer, and my eyes flutter closed just as his lips make contact with mine. His hands settle on my hips, fingertips lightly squeezing the soft flesh. Our kiss starts off soft and slow. Soon, though, it isn't enough, and I need more.

I tangle my fingers in the hair at the back of his head and pull him closer. His hands slip lower and squeeze my ass firmly, causing my hips to press into him. I can feel the length of his cock through his pants and how it twitches at the contact, making me shiver in response.

A faint growl rumbles up from his throat and he dips his hands lower, lifting me up in the air. I wrap my legs around his waist, and he presses my back against the wall. He breaks the kiss to trail hot, wet kisses down my neck, and I grind my hips against him, needing more pressure for the growing ache in my core.

"Bedroom." It's not a question. I need him on top of me. Now.

"You're already desperate for me, aren't you, baby?" His deep voice washes over me, sending another, almost painful, pulse of heat between my legs. "Don't worry, we'll get there. I'm going to take my time worshiping you and making you come all over this condo first. Just be a good girl and let me take it slow, I promise you'll enjoy it."

"Fuck that." I've been patient enough. "I need to come now, we can go slow later."

He groans and pulls me off the wall. "Have it your way, then."

19

Cameron

I carry her down the hall, never allowing my lips to leave her skin. She whimpers in my arms, so desperate for me. And I fucking love it. As we cross the threshold to my bedroom, Astrid pulls her shirt off over her head, exposing her gorgeous breasts covered in a sheer lace bra. The sight of her pert little nipples through the fabric distracts me, and I lose track of where we are in the bedroom, reaching the bed a step earlier than I expect and practically falling on top of her.

When I right myself, I remove my shirt, needing a moment to calm down. She might be frantic for this to happen quickly, but it's been so long since we last hooked up, I might go off like I rocket if I'm not careful. She's desperate for an orgasm, and I'm happy to deliver. I just need to make sure she's almost had enough before my cock joins the party.

Astrid sits on the edge of the bed and reaches for my belt, clearly determined to take this as fast and hard as she can. I grab her wrists before she's able to unfasten it and push her down onto the mattress. I lock both her small wrists in one of my hands above her head and settle down beside her. My cock throbs against her thigh and I push it harder against her. She shivers at the contact and arches her back.

The move lifts her breasts, drawing my attention down. I close my mouth over one pebbled nipple and suck through the fabric of her bra. The breathy sounds she makes remind me of how vocal she is in bed, and my cock responds with another painful throb. I snake a hand under her and unclasp her bra, pulling it down her arms and throwing it across the room. I move to the waistband of her jeans next, yanking them down and discarding them along with her panties in one motion.

A low grumble rises from my throat at the sight of her naked in my bed. My cock begs to be released from behind my zipper, but he's going to have to wait to come out and play.

"Fuck, you're stunning." Settling back down on top of her, I kiss down her soft skin to one bare breast. I suck her nipple deep into my mouth and knead the other breast, pinching the nipple hard and biting down on the other one before releasing it and sucking gently again to soothe it. She lets out the sexiest moan, and I nearly come in my pants.

"Cam," she says breathlessly, "I need you."

"Shhh baby. You just lie back and let me take care of you."

I continue to kiss down her torso, preparing her for where my mouth is going next. I find a sensitive spot right at her waist, at the base of her ribs. Kissing and nipping her there has her hips bucking into the air. I clamp my hands down on either side of her. I press my thumbs in firmly on the spots just below her hip bones, causing her to tilt her pelvis and giving me a fucking perfect view of her pussy, already dripping with anticipation.

"Fuck, you're so sexy." I turn my attention back to her torso. I press a kiss to her navel and dig my fingertips into the smooth flesh of her outer thighs.

"Cameron," she moans and pushes on the top of my head, trying to force me to go lower.

I chuckle. "Okay baby, I'll give you what you want."

I settle down lower, pushing her knees up and opening her up for me. I drag a finger through her arousal, and she lets out a groan.

"Already so wet for me," I say against her thigh, nipping at her smooth skin with my teeth. I kiss over to her center and give her a hard lick with the flat of my tongue from her entrance up to her clit.

Her hips buck and she moans again.

"Fuck, you taste amazing," I murmur against her clit.

She twists her fingers into the hair on top of my head, pulling hard.

"Please," she begs.

I seal my lips to her and suck hard on her clit. Her legs tremble as I dip a finger into her sweet pussy. I flick my tongue over her swollen clit, and she grinds up to meet me. I add another finger and curl them until I find the little spot inside her I know will make her come undone.

"Shit," she gasps, already on the edge of her climax.

I slow down. I want to draw this out and I'm not ready for her to come yet. An idea forms in my head. It's not anything we've talked about as off-limits, but with as aroused as she is, I might as well go for it.

I withdraw my index and middle fingers from her heat and replace it with my pinky. She doesn't seem to notice since I'm also trailing my teeth along her clit. I kiss a trail away from her clit and down to the spot I had my thumbs dug into earlier.

"You tell me to stop, and I'll stop," I say as I trail my pinky lower. I press it against her ass, and she gasps.

I replace my index and middle fingers in her pussy and go back to kissing and sucking on her clit. All the while, my pinky plays with her asshole, teasing and waiting for her to be ready.

Glancing up at her, I see she has one hand clamped onto her breast. I reach up and swat it away, taking over so she can relax. I can feel she's getting close, and I remember how wild her movements get when she comes.

Thinking about her coming has my cock impossibly hard. As much as I want to savor this, if I don't get my cock in her soon, I'm going to embarrass myself.

She rocks her hips against my face. "Don't stop," she breathes.

I release her breast to clamp my arm down across her lower abdomen, pinning her hips in place so I can guide her through the orgasm without her slipping away from me. The muscles in her legs tense up and I slowly sink my little finger into her ass.

"Oh my God, yes!" she screams.

She grabs my hair and holds my face against her as the orgasm slams into her. She comes hard and grinds against me as wave after wave of pleasure wash over her, my fingers pumping and guiding her through the ecstasy. I forgot how fucking hot she is when she comes. As she drifts back down to earth, I remove my fingers from her and give her clit one last flick with my tongue, for good measure.

She grabs the back of my neck and drags me up her body, sealing her mouth to mine. My face is slick with her come, and she laps it up. Her kiss is hungry and needy, like she didn't just have one of the most intense orgasms I've ever had the enjoyment of giving. I chuckle to myself at that. This woman drives me fucking wild, and I don't think I'll ever get enough.

20

Astrid

Cameron breaks our kiss suddenly. "Give me one second, okay?"

Before I can respond, he jumps up and goes into the bathroom. I hear the sink turn on. Tasting myself on his tongue was the most erotic thing I've ever experienced. Cameron is the only man I've been with that has made me feel this confident in bed. That feeling, surprisingly, is a huge turn on.

He exits the bathroom less than a minute later, finding me sprawled out on the bed with a hand between my legs.

"Please don't tell me you faked it and are in here trying to get yourself off." He lies down next to me, pulling me hard against him.

"If you couldn't tell that was real, then we may need to get you to a hospital because you may have had a stroke." I give him a kiss and moan, the taste of my orgasm lingering on his tongue.

Answering with a growl of his own, he presses his hips firmly against me and I can feel the throbbing of his cock against my thigh.

I expect him to push me away when I reach for his belt again. Instead, he just watches as I push his pants down his hips and his cock springs free. He kicks his pants off the rest of the way, and I rise to straddle him before he can make the first move. It's about damn time I have a little fun of my own.

His breathing is ragged as I kiss my way down his hard chest. He's built like a fucking Greek god and the way he fucks makes me feel like his goddess. As I continue kissing down his tight abs, I reach down and give his cock a firm stroke. As soon as I wrap my fingers around it, it pulses on its own.

"You see how hard you make me, baby?" His words echo my own thoughts.

While my lips continue to trail down his lean body, I swirl my thumb over the drop of moisture leaking from the tip. Finally, I flick my tongue over the head of his cock and his answering moan draws my eyes up to meet his.

His brows are knit together, mouth frozen in an open O, and his gaze is fixed on me. I give him another pump with my fist.

Keeping my eyes locked on him, I place my tongue flat against the base of his cock, right above his balls. Slowly, I drag my tongue up, giving him a swirl when I taste the salty bead of fluid at the tip.

He sucks in a breath between his teeth.

"*Fuuuck*," he rasps.

He reaches down and gathers my hair, pulling it back out of my face. I smirk, enjoying him being at my mercy. I close my lips around the head and suck gently while my hand pumps up from the base. He fists the hair at my nape but doesn't push me further down.

"Astrid," he moans.

I take his cock all the way to the back of my throat and seal my lips around his shaft. His grip on my hair tightens, and he pulls me off his cock and curses. Reaching down with his other hand, he grabs the back of my arm and hauls me up his body until we're face to face. He pulls my mouth to his and kisses me passionately.

"You can't do that and expect me not to embarrass myself," he mutters.

I open my mouth to protest. I want to keep going, but I'm suddenly underneath him again. He's kissing my neck, and his fingers trail down to circle my clit. I'm lost in the sensation and vaguely feel his weight shift as he reaches for the nightstand.

He tears open a condom packet with his teeth and lifts off me for half a second to roll it on. Then he's back, and the tip of his cock glides along my slick pussy. My eyelids flutter closed, and I let out a moan.

"Eyes on me, baby." He smooths my hair back out of my face.

I open my eyes to meet his and feel the tip of his cock nudge into me. I stiffen at the sheer size of him, and my breath seizes in my throat. I'd forgotten how much just the tip of him stretched me.

"Shhh, stay with me," he whispers.

He holds himself above me and kisses me gently, waiting for me to be ready for more. I wrap my legs around him and dig my heels into the backs of his thighs.

He snickers against my lips. "That's my girl."

He eases his cock deeper until he's fully seated. The sensation of being stretched sends electricity up my spine, and I gasp.

"Fuck," he pants. "I love how tight you are."

He pulls back almost all the way before driving back inside, hitting that sweet spot and taking my breath away. His pubic bone grinds against my clit, and my walls tighten around him even more.

He sets a slow, tantalizing pace. Each time the head of his cock approaches the spot deep inside me, he reverses and eases back out. My body is desperate for another release. I angle my hips to try to force him deeper.

"Please, Cam. I need more," I gasp.

He leans back and rests on his knees. He pulls my legs up and locks my ankles together on top of one of his shoulders. The change in position gives me the angle I need, but now my clit is missing out on the stimulation his pubic bone was giving. I reach down with one hand to rub my clit, and he catches my wrist before I can make contact.

"Not yet, baby."

I let out a frustrated groan—the pressure is building, and I need a release. I cinch my walls tighter around him, and he releases his own groan.

"Fuck it," he rumbles.

He unlocks my ankles and pushes my knees up, hitting both the angle and the depth my body craves. He places a hand right above my pubic bone and presses lightly on my stomach, increasing the pressure of his cock on the sweet spot deep inside me.

It only takes a few thrusts in that position for my orgasm to start to rise to the surface.

"Let go, baby. I want to feel your pussy milk my cock while you come," he murmurs into my ear.

His dirty words send me over the edge. My orgasm rips through me, and I dig my fingernails into his shoulders while I hold on for dear life. He curses and I feel the throbbing of his own release deep inside me.

We both float back down to earth, panting and slick with sweat. I open my eyes to look at him and he grabs the back of my head, lifting me to him for a deep kiss before he collapses on the bed next to me.

21

Cameron

Goddamn, that sex was amazing. I toss the condom onto the floor and collapse on the bed next to Astrid, totally spent. I don't think I've ever come that hard.

Astrid grabs me and kisses me like she's drowning and I'm her only source of oxygen. She presses her sexy body up against mine and I know she's ready for another round.

"That was amazing," she says against my lips.

"Mm-hmm," is the only response I can give because her mouth is already sealed back to mine.

"Let's do it again," she mutters, reaching for my cock.

I cup the side of her face and ease her back enough for me to be able to talk, which only causes her to kiss down my neck and nibble at my ear.

"Astrid, baby," I laugh, "I'm going to need a minute."

She sucks my earlobe into her mouth, and my cock twitches back to life. He's clearly on Astrid's side.

"I have tiramisu," I blurt out.

She pulls back and looks at me, eyes narrowed. "What?"

"There's tiramisu in the fridge from Danza Lento."

She blinks at me. "Why didn't you say something?"

"I would have if you didn't have a one-track mind." I laugh and reach up and pinch one of her nipples. "Unless you'd rather stay in bed."

She swats my hand away. "Nope. Let's do dessert." She jumps up and heads to the bathroom.

"Anyone ever tell you you're horrible for a guy's ego?" I laugh.

She scoffs and turns around in the doorway. "You've already got the biggest ego of any man I've ever met. You can handle it." She winks at me and closes the bathroom door.

The sound of my phone ringing drifts in from somewhere in the condo. Not thinking much of it, I throw on a pair of sweatpants and rummage around in my dresser for something small for Astrid to wear. Before I can find anything, the sound of my phone ringing again has me a bit worried. No one calls me unless it's important, let alone back-to-back.

I walk into the kitchen as my phone starts ringing for a third time.

Picking it up off the counter, I answer the call. "Jess, this better be good."

"Cameron! I'm so sorry to bother you. I know you had plans, and I wouldn't interrupt if it wasn't important." Her frantic voice has me even more worried.

"What's going on? Is everything okay?" My stomach drops.

"Some of your groceries got mixed with Justin's and ended up at his place. I need to bring them by. I'm sorry, it won't happen again, I swear."

The fuck? This is so out of character for her. Not only because she *never* makes mistakes like that, but also because she knows she never has to grovel. "Yeah, Jess. Groceries aren't really on my list of priorities at the moment."

I hear snickers in the background as Jess mumbles something that I can't make out, but I catch the words "bad at prank calls."

"Jess, who's there with you?" I ask, even though I'm pretty sure I already know the answer.

"Hey buddy!" Justin's voice comes through the speaker.

"What the fuck, dude? You know I'm busy."

More laughter. It doesn't sound like he's the only one of my teammates there. Probably at the bar they all like to frequent.

"Just wanted to check in and see how your date was going. Need any advice?"

"Goodbye, asshole."

"Wait, Cam!" Jess's voice comes back on the line. "I did mix up some of the things you said you want—"

Astrid wandering into the kitchen distracts me and I don't hear the last bit of what Jess is telling me. She's wearing my dress shirt from earlier and fuck if it isn't the sexiest thing I've ever seen.

"Cam? You there?" Jess's voice pulls my thoughts away from the vision in front of me.

"Yeah, sounds good." I hang up before I give the guys anymore material to razz me over.

Astrid motions to the phone. "Everything alright?"

"Just the guys being assholes." I toss my phone onto the counter. "You ready for some dessert?"

"Yes, please." She rubs her hands together excitedly.

I snort and motion to the cabinets behind her. "Can you grab us a couple plates out of that cabinet while I get the tiramisu out of the fridge?"

"Sure," she says, turning to face the wall of cabinets behind her.

I turn my attention to the fridge. I spot the tiramisu right away but rummaging around sparks my memory. What did Jess say? That she mixed up some groceries? I look through the shelves, surveying everything. I usually have her get the same things for me every week, but I spot one thing missing: eggs. Dammit. I wanted to make eggs Benedict for Astrid in the morning. Gonna be hard to do that without eggs. Maybe we'll go out instead. That is, of course, if she even wants to spend the night. We hadn't talked about it, and she didn't bring a bag. Is her purse big enough for a change of clothes?

Her frustrated grunts and the sounds of various cabinets being opened and closed repeatedly pull my attention back to the woman behind me. I grab the tiramisu and shut the fridge. Astrid is reaching up to look in one of the upper cabinets, arms raised high. The stance causes my dress shirt to ride up her toned legs, exposing the tantalizing curve of her ass and the little triangle gap between her legs that leads to one of my favorite places on earth.

I come up behind her and place my hands on her arms, bringing them down to rest flat on the counter. Brushing her hair over to one side, I kiss her neck. I wrap one arm around to her stomach and press her back into me, and she rolls her head to the other side, giving me more access to the sensitive spot right below her ear.

Using my free hand, I reach up to the adjacent cabinet and grab two plates, my lips never leaving the soft flesh of her neck. I give her ear a little nip with my teeth, and she squeaks. I huff out a laugh and step away from her, leaving the plates right in front of her on the counter.

She looks down at the plates and turns to me, frowning. "Where were those hiding?"

"They were in that cabinet you were looking in the whole time." I feign innocence, but a smile tugs at the corners of my mouth.

I plate up two huge portions of tiramisu and lead Astrid into the living room. Leaving the plates on the coffee table, I switch on the gas fireplace and the flames roar to life. It's not as nice as having a wood-burning fireplace, but it sure is convenient. I turn back around to see Astrid sitting on the huge couch, legs tucked neatly under her.

I sit close to her on the couch and pass her a plate.

She hums. "This is nice."

Her words hit me. Like really hit me. This *is* nice. I've never wanted to share my space with anyone. But with Astrid being here, this place feels less like a place I'm staying in between away games and more like... home.

"I'm really glad you're here." I smile back at her, place a hand on her thigh, and squeeze lightly. "Now, eat your dessert before I eat you instead."

She giggles and starts in on her dessert. Astrid looks out the windows at the twinkling city lights between bites and I, in turn, watch her. She's so beautiful. I was an idiot not to have pushed her in Vegas to give me some way to find her. Then again, if she had wanted to be found, she wouldn't have disappeared.

She must feel my eyes on her because a quizzical look crosses her features.

"What? Why are you looking at me like that?"

I shake my head, trying to dodge the thought, but I'm unsuccessful. "I'm just watching to see how the magician does her trick."

Despite trying to keep the mood light, I feel like I just took it in the opposite direction.

She stiffens. "What do you mean?"

I draw in a shaky breath. I guess it's time we dealt with the elephant in the room. "The last time we had sex, you disappeared on me. I didn't want it to end like that. I didn't expect you to regret our night together so much that you just ran away."

Her face screws up in a painful grimace.

"Cameron." She takes a deep breath. "I'm sorry I ran. Not that it excuses my behavior, but I was in an emotional state. I was hurting and I wasn't myself."

I hold up a hand, regretting taking us down this road. "You don't have to explain yourself. I get it."

She shrinks in on herself, making her already small frame look even smaller. "I don't think you do get it, though," she says so softly I almost miss it.

The sweet dessert turns sour in my stomach. Seeing her look so defeated has my heart cracking in two. How could anyone claim to love the vibrant woman I've only been lucky enough to catch glimpses of over the last couple of weeks and cut her down to the hollow shell I see before me?

I take her hand in mine and brush my lips over her knuckles. "Why don't you enlighten me, then?"

She wrinkles her nose. "You don't want to hear about my ex."

I lift her chin to meet my eyes. "Whatever happened between the two of you, it made you lose your fire. I don't want it to go out again, I want to stoke it and make it burn brighter than before. But in order to do that, I need to know what happened."

She lets out a shaky breath and nods. "Okay."

22

Astrid

I've fought like hell over the last several months to build myself back up to the confident woman I was before I met Landon. I owe it to Cameron to open up about my past. My fear, though, is that if I show Cameron my past, I'll also give him the power to take me back there.

I want to stoke it and make it burn brighter than before.

No man who says things like that can possibly be capable of pulling the rug out from under me. Cameron is different. He isn't Landon. I know deep down that he wouldn't do that.

And yet... There was a time when Landon said things that made me think he would never do what he did.

"If you don't want to tell me, you don't have to, but I am genuinely curious." He brushes his thumb over my bottom lip and gently coaxes it out from between my teeth. I hadn't realized I was biting it.

I take a deep breath, leaning into Cameron's touch as I tell him everything. About Landon's overbearing mother, who hated me. That he started telling me how to dress and act, how desperate I was for his approval and about his ever-changing standards I could never live up to. I tell him about my suspicions that he was seeing someone on the side, but every time I confronted him, he found a way to turn it around and make our fight my fault.

The memory of where I was mentally at that point in my life makes bile rise in my throat and I lean forward, resting my elbows on my knees as a wave of nausea washes over me. Cameron rubs gentle circles on my back as I focus on my breathing.

After several minutes, I finally sit back, relaxing a bit. Cam, who's sitting with rapt attention waiting for me to continue, reaches up and tucks a strand of hair behind my ear. He settles his arm on the back of the couch, his fingers drawing lazy circles on my shoulder.

"About a year and a half after we'd moved to Boston, he proposed. And I said yes, God knows why."

As I spill all the sickening details of the way Landon treated me, Cameron sits there and listens intently, the expression on his face morphing from neutral to disgust to sympathy. The more I share with him, the more I go from feeling trapped by my past to feeling like I'm setting myself free.

"One night, Bailey and I go to a different spot for girls' night. We ended up going to this swanky new bar downtown instead of our normal Mexican cantina in Back Bay. Landon was working crazy hours, helping with a high-profile trial for one of the senior partners. So, Bailey and I are sitting there drinking and talking shit about our boss, when in walks in the senior partner Landon had mentioned he'd be helping late at the office."

"What an idiot," Cam mutters.

Despite the awfulness of the story, I smile. "Oh, it gets worse."

Cam rolls his head back, groaning, and I laugh as I continue.

"Bailey convinces me that there is *not* a reasonable explanation for him being at the bar and I go home feeling like an idiot. When Landon came home, I confronted him with a picture I snapped of the partner from across the bar. He responded by threatening to call off the wedding, since I clearly didn't trust him. I had caught him in a lie and he expertly spun it around on me until I was begging and pleading with him for hours not to call off the wedding."

"Like he had never given you a reason to doubt him." Cam rolls his eyes and shakes his head. It's kind of nice to see him going all white knight for me. I think I might like it.

I huff out a breath. "Yeah. Not a moment I'm proud of. Anyway, the next morning at work, straight away Bailey could tell something had happened. I broke down, told her everything that happened, and she was ready to beat his ass."

Cam laughs. "I've always liked her."

I laugh too, remembering it was Bailey who pushed me to spend the night with Cam in Las Vegas. "She's the best. And as my best friend, she offered to cover a client pitch for me so I could go home and rest, even though I had only been at work for less than an hour. So, I went home. And I find women's clothing on the floor like breadcrumbs leading from the front door to our bedroom. I follow the trail like an idiot, even though I know what I'm about to find. Lo and behold, there's Landon, balls deep in one of the female partners from his firm. Exactly three months shy of our wedding."

Cam blows out a puff of air, the sudden rush of it reminding me to breathe myself.

"So, what did you do?" He looks like he's about to be sick on my behalf.

"It was so close to the wedding that I had no hope of getting any deposits back. Most of my savings had gone towards splitting the bill for various vendors since I refused to be any further under his parents' financial thumb. I needed a place to live and didn't have any of my own furniture, so I sold the only thing I could to get some quick cash."

"Which was..." Cam leads me.

I can't hold back my grin. Surprisingly, I'm excited to share this part of the story. "My engagement ring. Our matching wedding bands, too. I was going to use the money to furnish an apartment for myself. But I couldn't stand the thought of being surrounded by the things I only had money to buy because my relationship fell apart. So instead, I donated all of it."

Cameron's eyebrows shoot up. "Donated? To where?"

"To a free legal clinic that helps the victims of domestic violence divorce their abusers and start a new life."

His head rolls back as he laughs. "Oh, that's perfect."

A laugh bubbles up my throat. Telling this all to Cameron has been cathartic. "That's not even the best part. The next day, I got a call from the legal clinic explaining that since the donation was the largest they had ever received, it would be a wonderful opportunity for them if I would agree to a photo shoot so they could use it in advertising and fundraising. I agreed that *was* a wonderful opportunity, then gave them Landon and his mistress's names as the donors and the address of their law firm with instructions to show up there for the photo shoot. I assumed it would be maybe a couple people from the free clinic shaking their hands for a second to take a picture, but no. They showed up to his law firm with the clinic's entire team and several previous clients and one of those giant checks and invited his entire firm to be in the picture."

Cam can't contain his laughter as the sound of my own bubbles up and mixes with his.

"So, they take this picture and it's in total Publisher's Clearinghouse style, with balloons and everything. They put that picture on their website and have been using it in their fundraising campaigns ever since."

We both continue to laugh at the unwitting karma I doled out to my ex. Finally, our laughter dies down and we look at each other.

"I was wrong," he says softly.

I look at him, confused.

He cups the side of my face and brushes his thumb over my cheek. "He couldn't put out your fire. I knew you were stronger than that."

A smile plays at the corners of my mouth. I feel a sense of relief, like the power I allowed these events to hold over me just evaporated.

He pulls my mouth to his and kisses me. It soothes my inner turmoil like a balm to my soul.

When we separate, I feel renewed. The weight of my past no longer dragging me below the surface.

Cam presses his forehead to mine. “Stay with me tonight, Astrid.”

Another smile breaks out across my face. “Okay.”

23

Cameron

I think I've died and gone to heaven. That's the only logical explanation for me waking up here, after the best night of my life, lying next to the woman I lo—

Woah. No. Love? That can't be right.

Last night was a turning point. Astrid opened up to me about exactly what had happened with her ex. I'm so amazed by her strength. I wanted to spend every waking moment putting the pieces of her back together, but she isn't broken. She had already picked up the scattered fragments of herself long before she ever met me. She may not have all the pieces put back in their rightful places, but they're all present and accounted for.

After she shared all the ways in which her ex mistreated her, I spent the rest of the night fucking all those memories right out of her. I hope she realizes that I'm not at all like him. If she can take a chance and give me her heart, I'll treasure it and protect it every day for the rest of my life. Maybe it is love.

I've never seen myself settling down before. The nomadic lifestyle that comes with being a professional athlete has never allowed me to imagine it as a possibility for myself. But fuck, I would do anything to wake up every morning with her in my arms.

Astrid stirs and I pull her tighter against my body. I press a kiss to her hair, and she hums.

"Good morning, beautiful," I murmur into her ear. "Sleep well?"

She stretches and rolls over to face me, throwing one of her legs over mine.

"Mm-hmm, I'm still sleepy though. What time is it?"

I glance at the alarm clock on the nightstand. "It's only seven."

She scrunches up her beautiful face. "Gross. Do you always wake up this early on Saturdays?"

I snicker and nuzzle into her neck. "Stick around and find out."

She opens one eye and looks at me. "I don't know. Seven a.m. wake-up calls on the weekends might be a deal breaker for me."

"You'll get used to it."

"We'll see..."

A big, stupid grin spreads across my face, and not because I know she's joking. She just acknowledged that she sees a future with me. That feels better than winning the Stanley Cup.

I give her another squeeze. "I'll be in the guest room working out. You go back to sleep and when you wake up, we'll have breakfast."

"Mmmkay," she mumbles into the pillow and burrows herself deeper under the covers.

I get up, throw on a pair of sweatpants, and sit on the edge of the bed, watching her. She's already asleep again. After putting on my running shoes, I plant a kiss on her hair and head out of my bedroom, closing the door silently on my way out.

Heading to the guest room turned home gym, it finally hits me full force. I'm in love with her. I don't know how long I can hold off sharing how I feel, either. Even after the monumental step forward she took in trusting me last night, I don't want to spook her.

The pace I set on the treadmill is brutal. Normally, I would be exhausted after forty minutes of running at top speed, but for some reason, Astrid's presence here has me feeling more energized than usual.

After the treadmill, I move over to the small set of free weights and focus on my chest and back. Just a few reps in, I hear the front door open and close.

My first thought is that Astrid is awake and bailing on me. I should run after her, I want to, but I just sit there, feeling deflated. If she just left, I guess all the things I was feeling were simply one-sided. She doesn't feel the same.

I sink down on the bench and hang my head. Tears sting the backs of my eyes and I blink them away. I was an idiot to think that she was ready for a relationship. I should have just taken her disappearances in Vegas and at the bar at face value: she doesn't want to be with me.

I faint knock in the doorway jolts me from my thoughts and my head snaps up.

"Jess? What are you doing here?"

Jess looks at me, confused. "Your groceries. We talked about this last night. Are you alright?"

I avoid her question. "Did you see anyone leaving on your way in?"

"Uh no, why?"

"Just curious."

She eyes me warily. "If you're worried that your guest left, she's sleeping. I assume so, at least, since your bedroom door is closed and you're in here."

Relief floods me. "It is?" I ask, standing from the bench.

"Yeah? Anyway, I'm going to put away your groceries real quick and get out of your hair."

I pick up the weights again, feeling nearly as good as I did a minute before Jess got here. "Sounds good. Thanks, Pete."

She rolls her eyes at the nickname, and I laugh to myself as she turns to leave. I can't even remember now how she got it, but I do remember she absolutely hates it. Naturally, Justin and I use it on her at every opportunity.

I get my lifting routine back underway and only manage a few reps before a blood-curdling shriek has me sprinting to the kitchen.

My first thought is that Jess somehow cut herself. Not that it would warrant a scream like that.

My next thought is that—

Astrid.

I come to a screeching halt when I get to the kitchen and see Jess, standing there dumbfounded with her hands raised in innocence. Astrid vibrates with rage, vitriol darkening her normally light features.

The way she looks like she's about to tear me limb from limb terrifies me, but I'm so incredibly turned on by the fact that she's wearing my dress shirt. My dick is only focusing on how sexy she is, totally oblivious to the fact Astrid looks like she wants to chop him off.

"Astrid." I edge toward her and put my hands up in a gesture meant to calm her.

She turns to face me, and I see tears brimming in her deep emerald-green eyes.

I inch closer to Astrid. "This is Jess. She's my assistant."

I'm treating her like she's a fucking lion at the zoo, ready to pounce. If she was anywhere near as livid as this when she walked in on her ex in the act with another woman, I can only imagine the hell she raised.

Astrid's head snaps to Jess, who gives a very timid wave, accompanied by a nervous smile.

"I'm going to go." Jess motions toward the door.

I nod and she bolts. Then it's just Astrid and me. I swallow hard, hoping I can smooth this over.

Slowly, I continue my slow approach. "Astrid, baby, let me explain."

She stands stock still, chest heaving, eyes watching me. "Please do." The ice in her words pierces my heart.

I'm standing directly in front of her now, and I place my hands on her upper arms. "Jess is my assistant. And Justin's little sister."

Astrid continues staring at me, which I take as a sign that it's safe for me to continue.

"I've known her since we were kids. She might as well be my own little sister. She was only here to drop off a few things from the store."

She blinks for the first time in a full minute. "So, you've never slept with her."

I cup her face in my hands and wipe the tears that spill over. "No, *never*. Please believe me when I tell you, I never would. Not with anyone. Not ever. I lo—" I stop myself, blowing out my breath before I can say the words.

Astrid looks up at me with wide, doe-like eyes. The hint of a smile flashes across her features.

"You... what?" she asks breathlessly.

I lean down and bring my forehead to hers. I close my eyes and take a deep breath. No more waiting. She needs to hear this as much as I need to say it. "I love you."

She lets out a puff of air, and I open my eyes, bracing myself to defend my feelings for her.

"Astrid, I know it's only been a short time, but I'm not going to try to hide the way I feel about you."

"Cameron," she starts, and I cringe, dropping my hands and standing up to my full height again.

"I'm not just saying this now because you thought I was stepping out on you. It's true. I tried to fight it but I can't hold it back anymore. I'm in love with you."

"Cam—"

"Baby, it's okay. You don't have to say it back."

"Cameron." She reaches up and grabs my jaw, forcing me to look at her. "I love you, too."

I huge grin spreads across my face, and my chest feels like it's just burst open. Wrapping my arms tightly around her, I lift her up and spin her around. She giggles and squeals, and when I set her back on her feet, she looks up at me, cheeks flushed and breathless.

God, I love this woman so much it hurts. And now she's mine. I grab her and kiss her ferociously. Her tongue darts out of her mouth to meet mine, and I'm desperate to show her just how much it means to me to have her love in return.

I stoop slightly to hook my hands under her ass and lift her up, setting her on the marble countertop of the kitchen island. She gasps as the cold stone shocks her skin. Trailing kisses down her neck to the tiny bit of her exposed collarbone, I slowly run my hands up her thighs.

“Say it again,” I say, my voice thick with desire.

“I love you.”

She no sooner says the words than I give the shirt a quick jerk, popping all the buttons. I pepper her chest with hot, wet kisses, trailing a path lower until I close my mouth over one nipple and suck hard.

She fists her hands into my hair, holding my head against her as I lave my tongue over her peaked nipple. I slide the shirt down her shoulders and off her arms and give her shoulders a slight push. She lies back, and I place the balled-up shirt underneath her head as a makeshift pillow.

My attention zeros in on the thin layer of cotton covering her pretty little pussy. She places her heels on the edge of the counter and lifts her hips up so I can slide them down her long, slender legs.

I throw her legs over my shoulders and admire the goddess sprawled out before me. She’s already dripping with anticipation, and my cock aches to be buried inside of her. I flatten my tongue and give her a long, languid lick from her opening to her clit.

She lets out a loud moan as I sink two fingers deep inside her pussy. I finger fuck her on my countertop as my tongue draws tiny circles around her clit. I feel her getting close, so I slow my motions and bring her back from the edge of her orgasm.

My thumb replaces my mouth on her clit, and I trail kisses all over her. Down her thigh and back up again, over the small rise of her hip bone, across the taut skin of her lower abdomen, all while gently increasing the speed of my thumb on her clit. When I reach the other thigh, I bite down and she moans.

I feel her orgasm approaching again. "Not so fast, baby," I say as my movements bring her back away from the pleasure she's now so desperate for.

Good, I want to hear her beg for it.

"Fuck, Cameron! Please!" she screams.

Well shit, hearing that just about brought on my own orgasm. I hush her, trailing kisses up her body to her breasts. I nip at her tightly pebbled nipples, and she gasps.

"Need your cock," she croaks out, desperate.

I trail my kisses back down her body, staggering my words between kisses and curling my fingers deep inside her to stroke the spot that will make her see stars.

"First." Kiss.

"Come." Kiss.

"On." Kiss.

"My." Kiss.

"Face."

With the last word, I suck her swollen clit deep into my mouth and set a relentless pace with my fingers pumping in and out of her pussy. Without releasing suction, I flick my tongue against her clit, and she cries out.

The intense orgasm slams into her. The only thing she has to brace herself against is my hair, and she closes her fists in it and pulls so hard I think she might leave a bald patch. She rides it out like a fucking champ.

I love the way she looks right after she comes, eyes hooded and dark, a gentle flush across her chest, up her neck and across her cheeks. I give her clit one last flick of my tongue and she shudders.

She pulls me up to her by my hair and seals her mouth to mine. At the same time, her hand dives below the waist of my sweatpants and closes around my rock-hard cock. I groan into our kiss and push my pants down, kicking them to the side. She pumps my cock, and I shamelessly thrust into her fist.

"I want you to fuck me, right here," she purrs.

"I don't have a condom out here, baby. Let me take you to the bed," I say while kissing down her neck.

She squeezes my cock tighter in her fist. "Fuck the condom, I want you bare."

Surprised, I snap my head up, searching her eyes for a hint of amusement, but there is none.

"Astrid—"

"I'm on the pill and I'm clean. I got tested after everything with my ex. I haven't been with anyone but you since then."

I continue watching her, waiting for the other shoe to drop, but it doesn't.

She shrinks back from me an almost imperceptible amount. "What?"

Swallowing over the sand that's suddenly coating my throat, I find my words again. "I'm clean, too, but I've never gone raw before." The thought of slipping into Astrid with nothing separating us has my cock throbbing in her hand.

"So, let's make this a first for both of us," she pleads.

I cup the back of her neck and press my forehead to hers. "Are you sure?" I'm only going to ask her once.

She teases the tip of my cock against her slick heat, making me shudder. "I'm sure."

I swallow her words with an urgent kiss. Hooking my arms under her legs, I guide her hips closer to the edge of the countertop and line myself up with her opening. Gently, I press the tip of my cock into her. Our eyes lock on the place our bodies are joined.

When half my length has disappeared inside her velvety heat, I reverse my movements and slowly withdraw. *Shiiit*. I'm not going to last very long at all. I knew my ninth-grade health teacher was lying—sex does *not* feel the same without a condom. Astrid's pussy is tighter, hotter, wetter, smoother, more... everything. Knowing that when I finally give in to the sensations of her walls rippling around my cock, I'll come buried deep inside her instead of into a condom turns me on like nothing else ever has before.

Astrid's breathing is heavy and labored. She lets out a loud gasp when I press my cock a little deeper inside this time, going a little more than halfway in, feeling her walls tug at me, trying to pull me further inside. Again, I reverse out of her slowly, until I'm completely out.

This time when I press into her, I place my thumb on her clit and start tracing gentle circles, just to test her. Astrid moans and I feel her walls clamp down my cock so hard I nearly see stars.

"Fuuuuuck," I groan. "You feel so fucking good, baby."

She lifts her mouth to mine. We kiss as I set a lazy pace, my thrusts gentle and slow. I feel like I'm going to burst already, but I'm determined to make her come on my cock first. In no time at all, I feel my restraint start to slip as Astrid's orgasm creeps up on us.

I throw one of her legs up onto my shoulder, hooking my arm under her opposite knee and holding her leg out to the side. I pick up the pace, thrusting harder and harder. Fighting off my orgasm, I trail kisses down Astrid's neck.

"Oh my God, yes!" she cries out, teetering on the edge of her release.

"That's it, baby. Be a good girl and come for me."

Her legs suddenly go stiff and her pussy locks like a vise around my cock as her pleasure builds, like a dam about to fracture. The moment it bursts, I feel the walls of her pussy tremble and quiver, and then I'm following her over the edge myself. My balls tighten and I feel electricity sizzle in my spine. Then I burst and my cock throbs as pulse after pulse of my come shoots into her, mixing with her own release.

My thrusts continue through both our orgasms, only slowing when we've slipped back to earth.

"That was incredible." I'm breathless, spent, and I've never been more satisfied.

"Oh my God. That was amazing," she replies, in almost an identical state of exhaustion.

I slowly glide my cock out of her, watching raptly as some of my come drips out of her and onto the counter.

"Don't move." I cross to the other side of the kitchen and grab a clean hand towel out of a drawer. I run some warm water over it so it doesn't shock her and return to my spot between her legs.

I wipe up the rest of the come that has dripped down her ass, and I catch her smiling at me.

"Thank you," she says sweetly.

"Anything for you." And I mean it.

24

Astrid

I sit on Cameron's enormous couch, waiting for him to get home from his game. I could have gone, but I didn't want to go by myself, and I knew Bailey had plans with a Tinder date. Instead, I sat in front of Cameron's huge gas fireplace, ordered a ton of takeout for myself, and cheered on the Bears to victory.

This morning, after we had sex on his kitchen island, we showered together. I was blow-drying my hair—and trying not to think about the last person who might have stayed here who needed a hair dryer—and he made a comment about how much he hated that his schedule got in the way of us spending time together. I had offered to meet up with him for lunch tomorrow, before the team left for their away games this week. Wrapping me in his arms, he had pretended to mull over my offer and came up with his own.

"How about this," he had said. *"You hang out here while I'm gone, and when I get back..."* His gaze swept down from my face to my legs and back up again.

Obviously, I accepted his offer. I was only expecting to spend last night here, so just packed one spare outfit. He drove me all the way to my apartment in Somerville to get a change of clothes. Then we went to one of my favorite brunch spots, a little crepe restaurant that has over fifty different combinations of sweet and savory fillings. The portion size is big enough to satisfy a professional hockey player's appetite, too.

So that's how I ended up here, waiting for Cameron to come back home. I feel a little bit like a pet, obediently waiting for his return. I swore I would never put myself in the position to feel secondary to the person I'm with, and that's how I should feel at this moment. But I don't. Cam has never made me feel like I come second to anything. He doesn't just want me here to have someone to come home to after his game. He wants me here because I'm *me.*

I look down at his jersey and pick off a stray piece of hair. While he was gone, I stripped out of every other piece of clothing and until only his jersey remained. He hasn't made good on his promise yet, and I intend to hold him to it.

The lock clicks and my stomach flips with anticipation. He's home. The sound of heavy footsteps drift in through the doorway that leads to the front door. A second later, Cameron's huge body fills up the door frame and our eyes lock.

Relief flashes over his face, and a smile blooms across his features.

"Hi, honey. I'm home." His voice is smooth and calm and doesn't betray the nervousness he must have been feeling as he entered his silent condo a moment ago.

I rise off the couch to greet him. The jersey is long enough that it covers my butt, so he has no idea that it's the only thing I'm wearing.

"Hey." Throwing my arms around his neck, I feel the hem of the jersey ride up to expose the curve where my ass and thighs meet. "That was an exciting game."

The game had been tied for most of the third, and Justin scored the winning goal just seconds before the period ended.

He hums. "Not nearly as exciting as coming home to you in my jersey."

His hands trail down my back to my ass and he gives a squeeze. He covers my mouth in a kiss before realizing his fingertips are touching bare skin. He lifts the jersey up higher, to where the waistband of my panties should be, and groans into our kiss when he finds nothing.

"Especially if my jersey is the only thing you're wearing," he says against my lips. He dips and throws me over his shoulder and starts toward the bedroom.

"Hey!" I shriek. "Put me down!" I beat my fists against the coiled muscles of his back with no effect. "What about what you said about doing it from behind on your couch while I'm wearing your jersey?"

I jump as his palm comes crashing down on the bare skin of my ass, replaced a second later by the soothing warmth of his caress.

"I already fucked you outside of my bed once today. I'm not about to do it again," he says darkly.

He swings me down on the floor of the bedroom, right in front of the floor to ceiling windows. He steps in close, forcing me back into the cold glass. A shiver runs through me, but not from the chill. Cameron has a feral gleam in his eyes, forcing me to wonder what he's got planned next.

He pushes my hair out of my face, and I feel his cock digging into my stomach through his dress pants. He places a hand on the glass on either side of my shoulders, caging me, and leans in.

"I love seeing my name on your back, baby," he says against the shell of my ear. "You can feel how hard it makes me, can't you?" His cock pulses on cue.

Mesmerized, I nod.

"Did you know how hard seeing you wear nothing but my jersey would make me?"

I nod again.

"So, you did it on purpose, then?"

Again, I nod.

He laughs darkly. "Well, sweetheart, get on your knees and check out your handiwork."

I do as he says and unclasp his belt. From the glow of the city lights coming in through the windows at my back, I can already see the hard outline of his erection. I push his pants down his legs, his cock springing free. He steps out of them, kicking them off to the side at the same time as he whips his shirt off over his head, without undoing the buttons.

My mouth waters to see him like this. Rock hard for *me*. I do this to him. Emboldened, I grab the base of his shaft and give him a few strokes while looking up at him through my lashes.

His eyes are locked on my mouth, telling me what my next move is. My tongue drifts out to lap up the bead of fluid that sits at the tip. I'm rewarded with a satisfying ripple of his abs.

I point his cock upwards and lean in close. I start at the base of him and slowly draw my tongue up the entire length of his cock. When I get to the tip, I cup his balls with one of my hands.

A soft curse slips from his mouth as I circle the crown of his cock with my tongue. I suck him into my mouth, forcing my throat to relax and take him deeper, past the resistance that wants me to stop.

He rewards me with a sharp breath and another ripple of his ab muscles. I keep working him deeper and deeper into my throat with every stroke until my nose brushes against the soft skin above his shaft.

"Oh *fuuuuuck,*" he groans, fisting his fingers in my hair. "You take me so good, baby."

His words send a thrill through me. I reach down and brush a finger over my swollen and throbbing clit.

"Are you wet, baby?" he asks.

"Mm-hmm," I answer, taking him all the way in my mouth to the base again.

"Finger yourself while you suck on my cock."

I do as he says, and in no time, I'm getting close to my climax. He pulls me up to him and kisses me fiercely.

"Rub your juices all over my cock before I fuck you," he says.

I take him in my hand and wipe all the wetness from my pussy onto his cock. He lifts me up. I seal my mouth to his as I wrap my legs around him, and he carries me to the bed.

He tosses me down and covers my body with his. I can feel the weight of his cock against my stomach, and I arch my hips, trying to get him closer to where I so desperately want him.

He expertly flips me over, grabs hold of my hips, and slams into me from behind. The shock of being suddenly filled by him is almost enough to make me come apart.

He reaches around to circle my clit with one hand. "I told you I wanted to fuck you from behind while you wore this and I'm so happy you decided to be a good girl and listen."

I gasp, both from his words and from the orgasm that is barreling toward me.

"Don't hold back, baby. Come hard for me."

I cry out as wave after wave of pleasure rocks through me. Cameron's thrusts grow more erratic as he chases his own release. He leans down over me, biting my shoulder through the fabric of his jersey, and his cock throbs and pulsates as he follows me over the edge.

***

Sunlight drifting in from the floor to ceiling windows wakes me. I squeeze my eyes closed, not wanting to face the day yet, and pull the covers up to my chin. Memories from last night come back to me in flashes. Cam taking me from behind, pulling my hair and biting my shoulder. Remembering the feeling of his thick cock filling me up and stretching me makes me clench my thighs together.

I roll over, expecting to find Cam, who has somehow disentangled himself from me during the night. When I don't feel him, I open my eyes and see that I'm alone. I sit up and listen for any clues as to where he might be. Soft kitchen sounds and the faint smell of bacon drifts in from the open doorway.

He's making breakfast.

I throw on one of Cam's tee shirts and pad out to the kitchen. I find him standing at the stove, his back to me. He's not wearing a shirt, and his sweatpants hang low on his hips. I watch as he moves and the hard muscles of his back and shoulders ripple and flex. Once again, the butterflies that have taken up residence in my stomach take flight.

He turns suddenly to grab a plate from the island and spots me. A smile breaks out across his face. He abandons the plate and rounds the kitchen island, pulling me into his arms.

"Good morning, beautiful," he says against my hair.

I tip my head back to look up at him. "Morning, handsome."

He presses a soft kiss to my lips before releasing me and returning to the stove.

"There's coffee in the pot, if you'd like some."

"I would, thanks. How long have you been up?" I begin searching through cabinets for a mug.

He glances over his shoulder, seeing my struggle, and chuckles. "Not long." He crosses the kitchen and opens the cabinet next to me, grabbing a mug and setting it down on the counter in front of me.

I blink at the mug, and Cameron wraps his arms around me again. "Okay, seriously, who needs this many cabinets?"

He kisses the tip of my nose. "You'll learn where everything is, eventually. Although, the more time you spend here, the faster you'll learn."

I harrumph at him, and he snickers, releasing me to continue cooking while I pour my coffee.

The next item I go in search of is some creamer. I'm usually a fan of the artificially flavored kind, but as I root around in the fridge, I'm not seeing any. Not even plain half and half.

I straighten, feeling the warmth of his hand on the center of my back. He leans into the open fridge around me and grabs a bottle of caramel flavored creamer from the back of the fridge. He hands it to me, clearly fighting off his sheer amusement at the situation.

"You better go ahead and drink that coffee, baby. You seem like you could use it." He pokes at the ticklish spot on my ribs.

After adding creamer to my mug, Cameron hands me a spoon before I can even go in search of one. I glare at him.

"Oh stop, you know you love me." His eyes gleam at me.

My face betrays me, and a smile breaks out at one corner of my mouth. "I do love you," I say, giving my coffee a stir.

"I love you, too, gorgeous," he replies over his shoulder, now back in front of the stove.

"So, what are you making? It smells amazing." I sidle up to the kitchen island on a barstool, watching him move effortlessly.

"Eggs Benedict with bacon. I wasn't sure if you preferred sausage or bacon, so I just picked one."

"Bacon is perfect for me, thank you." That was so thoughtful. Everything about this man is so wholesome and thoughtful. It's not something I'm used to in a relationship, and I can't shake the feeling that the other shoe is just waiting to drop. This is a good dynamic we have, and I might not be able to crawl up out of another pit of despair if this goes south.

25

Cameron

Waking up next to Astrid has become my new favorite thing. Besides fucking her, of course. She's so goddamned beautiful when she's sleeping. Don't even get me started on how sexy it is to see the woman you just spent hours fucking come wandering out to your kitchen all sleepy-eyed and in one of your shirts. *Lord have mercy.*

I quickly assemble the eggs Benedict while she watches me from the island. The thought of what we did twenty-four hours ago has desire coiling its way down my spine and straight to my balls. I ate her out then fucked her bare right in this very spot.

Shaking my dirty thoughts from my head, I grab silverware and napkins and carry the plates to Astrid. I set our plates down, squeezing between her and the barstool next to her, and face her. I'm standing too close, and her gaze rakes over my bare chest and abs. I smirk. I love knowing I have the same effect on her as she has on me.

"Buon appetito," I say when her eyes finally lift back to mine. I sit next to her and rest my arm across the back of her barstool.

She takes a bite and I'm treated to one of Astrid's trademark closed-eye moans with the first bite of food. The sight of her lips closing around her fork reminds me of something else she had her lips wrapped around last night. The object in question stirs to life in my pants at the thought.

She was so eager to have my cock in her mouth. I've never been with a woman who was so turned on by the thought of sucking my cock before. Then again, I'm turned on just by how much she's turned on. It's a vicious cycle of horniness. Maybe that's why our sex is the best of my life.

Even before we got to know each other, back in Vegas, the sex was incredible. I think back to that night when I ate her out while she sucked me off. *Fuck.* Now I'm at full mast. Forget breakfast, I need to fuck Astrid again.

I've been distracted by my dirty thoughts and have only taken a couple bites when I notice Astrid scraping up the last crumbs from her plate with her fork. *Perfect.*

She pushes her plate away and wipes her mouth with her napkin. "That was delicious."

I stand and cup the back of her neck with my hand, pulling her to me. I cover her mouth with a kiss and her hands twist into my hair. I don't think I'll ever grow tired of this woman.

She turns in her seat, allowing me to step between her legs. Our kiss turns urgent, and soon I'm fucking her mouth with my tongue. Her nails dig into my shoulders, and she scrapes them down my chest and over my abdomen. We're clearly on the same page here.

I reach down and cup her firm ass in the palms of my hands and lift her out of her seat. She wraps her legs around me, and I head back down the hallway to the bedroom. She whips her shirt off on the way, making me salivate at the sight of her gorgeous tits.

When my knees bump into the foot of the bed, I toss her down, and she scoots toward the pillows. I stalk up the bed toward her, reaching out and yanking her back down to me by her ankles.

She lets out a shriek of excitement at my sudden roughness, sending a thrill down my spine. My cock aches to be inside her, and I don't have enough restraint to take my time with her. Our time together today is already running short, and I've got to prioritize.

I cage her in with my body and kiss a trail down her neck, making her whimper. *Fuck, that's sexy*. I continue to trail kisses down her chest until I close my mouth over one tit, sucking her hard little nipple deep into my mouth.

She gasps and pulls my hair, so I scrape my teeth across her sensitive flesh over to her other breast and do the same thing. I reach down and run my fingers through her folds and groan.

"Already so wet for me," I murmur against her skin.

"I need you," she rasps.

She doesn't need to beg me today. I'll give her exactly what she wants without having to ask twice.

I line myself up with her sweet pussy and gently ease inside. She's so velvety smooth, hot, and tight that I see stars.

"Oh *fuck,* Astrid." I gasp. "I won't be able to go slow."

"Then don't," she bites out, breathless.

Fuck. Let's do this. I set a ruthless cadence. This isn't the slow, sensual love we made last night. This is urgent and desperate. Both of us using the other, racing to our orgasms, driven to ecstasy by each other's breathless pants and moans.

I fight off my orgasm, waiting for Astrid to go over the edge first. Her eyes close, mouth hanging open, and I know she's close.

I rise above her and push her knees back toward her head. My thrusts turn savage as I nail her into the mattress.

"Need you to come. Now." I choke out the words as I feel my balls tighten.

And then we're falling over the edge together, our cries muffled when our mouths find each other, and we both implode.

***

I glance down at my ringing phone and frown.

"Everything okay?" Astrid asks me in the mirror.

We just got out of the shower, and I'm already dressed and ready to go. I've been leaning against the bathroom doorframe, watching Astrid get ready for the last few minutes. I could watch her do anything and be fascinated.

"Fine." I hold up my phone. "I'm going to go take this."

She nods and I swipe to answer the call, heading out to the living room for a little privacy.

"Yeah," I answer, annoyed that this is taking my time away from Astrid.

"Mr. Grant, this is Detective Mathis with the Detroit Police. Do you have a minute to talk?"

"Yes, but make it quick, I'm in the middle of something," I say curtly.

"I wanted to let you know that we've allocated additional security ahead of your time in Detroit this week, and I can assure you, there won't be any security breaches." The detective's voice is deep and calming, like he's used to delivering this type of news and the person on the other end just accepting it. But I'm not that type of person.

"Good. It'll be your ass on the line if there are." I hang up without saying goodbye.

This is something I've not discussed with Astrid. I've been meaning to, but I keep avoiding it. A woman has been stalking me all over the Midwest since I hooked up with her in Chicago close to two years ago. She told me she was fine with us just being a hookup and that she wasn't looking for anything more. But in the morning, she was convinced we were in love. Since then, she's popped up anywhere within a ten-hour drive of Chicago, forcing me to file restraining orders in six different states. It was because of her antics that I hadn't hooked up with anyone after her until I met Astrid last summer.

Last February, she carried out an elaborate plan to sneak past security in Detroit. She took a guided tour of

Little Caesar's Arena the day before our game, broke off from the tour group, and hid in the away team's locker room overnight. The fact that no one noticed she broke off from the group was understandable. The tour guide was a minimum wage employee who had only been on the job a few days and had too much responsibility placed on them with too little experience. The security team is who I hold responsible. They should have cleared the locker room, especially when our general manager gave them the heads up about my stalker and her propensity to show up unexpectedly.

Rage bubbles up my throat at the helplessness of my situation. I can't have her arrested because she doesn't pose enough of a threat. I sit on the edge of the couch and lean forward, elbows on my thighs and head hanging. Truth be told, she doesn't pose a threat, but the psychological toll her presence in my life has taken over the last year has forced me to operate on pure anxiety while I'm on the road, at least in the Midwest. To date, she hasn't traveled farther than that, but I don't know what's stopping her. She could easily pop up here in Boston and cause utter chaos.

"Is everything okay?"

My head snaps up at the sound of Astrid's voice. "Hey, yeah." I shake off my thoughts and rise off the couch. I reach for Astrid and pull her into my arms. "Everything's fine."

I bury my face in her messy waves, inhaling the clean scent of shampoo.

She pushes back to look me in the eye. "Are you sure?"

This is it. My chance to be upfront with her. It's not a big deal. Plenty of people have stalkers. Astrid is a reasonable person, she'll understand, but the words die in my throat.

"Yeah, just something about our travel later." It's not a complete lie, but I still feel like shit for not telling her the truth.

She eyes me suspiciously, and for a second, I don't think she's going to buy my excuse. But she graciously gives me an out.

"Are you ready to go?" she asks.

I step back from her, patting the pockets of my jeans to make sure I have my wallet and keys.

"Yeah, let's go."

We both throw on our jackets and head out the door. She reaches for my hand as we wait for the elevator and the rest of my anxiety surrounding the stalker situation dissolves away. We continue holding hands until we're at the revolving door of the lobby and exiting onto Avery Street.

As soon as we're outside, Astrid hooks her arm through mine. For being mid-November, the sun is surprisingly warm. It could almost be mistaken for an early spring day if I didn't know any better. She breathes in the crisp fall air and snuggles into my side as we wait for the light to cross Tremont Street and enter Boston Common.

This time of year, there's not much going on at either the Common or the adjacent Public Garden. The fun of summer wrapped up for the year long ago and the weather is not yet cold enough to welcome the winter activities.

We walk together, neither of us bothered by the silence. Just enjoying being together. We make our way through the winding paths of the Common, passing by the Central Burying Ground before crossing Charles Street and entering the Public Garden.

The pond at the center of the Garden is a quiet, tranquil spot in the bustling city, even when packed with tourists during the summer travel season. But now, being the only two people here, I feel like I'm seeing it for the first time again.

We stop at the middle of the suspension bridge and look out at the ducks and geese floating on the still surface.

"What a life they lead," I say wistfully.

Astrid looks over at me and nods. "Must be nice to hang out on the water all day and eat your weight in bugs and fish."

I huff out a laugh, her joke not quite enough to pull me out of my sudden melancholy. "Do you ever think about what you would be doing if you weren't in your current profession?"

Her eyebrows shoot up. "No, I can't say I have."

"I do." I take a deep breath and blow it out. "A lot, actually."

"Why is that?" she asks.

I mull it over for a moment. "I've played in the NHL for nine years now. I'm incredibly successful and likely won't have to worry about money or finances ever. People recognize me, kids look up to me. On paper, it's everything I ever wanted out of life."

She eyes me. "And off paper?"

I shrug. "It's not at all what I wanted out of life. My one sister is married with a kid on the way, and the other is engaged to a great guy. I look at their lives and see what I've always wanted for myself. Not the penthouse or the fame. I would give all that up today if it meant I could lead the life I want starting tomorrow."

She turns to me and reaches up to touch my face. "You can be proud of your success and still wish for something different for your life. Just because you're extremely successful in one aspect doesn't mean you aren't allowed to want something in another area of your life."

I shake my head. "I've just been so fucking alone, you know? I'm constantly surrounded by people and my success, but if I don't have anyone to share it with, then what's it all for?"

She shrugs and looks up at me from under her lashes. "Maybe you could share it with me."

"I never really pegged you for someone who wanted a white picket fence," I say jokingly. My heart is soaring that she's willing to take on a crazy life with me, but at the same time, I've never gotten the sense that was the kind of life she wanted.

She hums. "I prefer cabin in the mountains, but"—she shrugs again—"why not?"

I square my shoulders with her to look her in the eyes, searching for any hint of reservations.

"Astrid," I say, taking her hands in mine, "I love you. I'm not about to ask you to marry me and commit to me for the rest of our lives, but I want to know that we're moving in that direction. Before we spend any more time together. I want to know that we both want the same things. Marriage. Commitment. I'll give you dogs, cats, babies, anything you want. I can see myself having all of that with you. I just need to know *you* want it, too."

Her emerald eyes bore into me for a split second before they soften and a smile spreads across her face. "Cameron, of course I want those things. And I want them with you, too."

"Really?" I feel like this must be a prank. Surely, the woman who's first instinct was to disappear on me in a Vegas hotel isn't the same one standing in front of me telling me that one day, she could be my wife.

"It shouldn't come as a surprise to you that I'd like to get married someday. Right now, I think you're the man who I could see a future with. Not that I'm ready to go down to the courthouse today." She laughs.

I wrap my arms around her and lift her off her feet, twirling her around in the air. Her giggles bring my own laughter to the surface.

I set her down and place both my hands on either side of her face. "I love you so much, Astrid."

"I love you, too, Cameron."

I press my lips to hers and savor the taste of this moment. Everything is right in the world. All the pieces have finally fallen into place.

Still reveling in the rush of the moment, I don't immediately notice a stranger approaching us. He looks to be about college-aged and he's holding an old Polaroid-style camera.

"Hi there," he calls from several feet away, not wanting to interrupt. "I'm a student at Boston University and I'm a photography major. I hope you guys don't mind, but I snapped a couple of candid pictures of you." He holds out a couple of Polaroids that haven't developed yet and are still mostly brown.

Astrid takes them from him, while I'm still trying to decide if this kid is a total psychopath.

"I'm not crazy or a creep or anything. I'm just out here for my class, trying to find some inspiration. Those are the only ones I took, I swear." He holds up one hand defensively.

Astrid nods. "Thank you. That was really sweet." She doesn't sound convinced.

"Enjoy the rest of your day," he says before hurrying off the way he came.

We both heave a sigh of relief. What a weird encounter.

"Do you want to get out of here?" I ask.

"Yes, immediately."

We head in the opposite direction from the camera kid, back in the direction of my condo. When we're safely out of the Public Garden and back on Charles Street, I turn to Astrid.

"Can I drive you home?" I'm not ready to say goodbye to her just yet.

"Don't you have to get to the airport?"

"Your place is on the way."

She blinks in confusion, then laughs. "No, it isn't."

I laugh, too. "Okay fine. I'm not ready to leave you just yet." I bend my knees slightly and stick out my bottom lip. "Please?"

She sighs. "You know you don't need to be my knight in shining armor, right?"

"I was hoping I could be more of an assistant to the magician."

She throws her head back in laughter. "I'm never going to live that down, am I?"

"Not as long as I'm around." I pull her in for a chaste kiss. "Let's get you home."

***

Coming back to an empty hotel room is the absolute worst. One game down, one to go on the road until I can see Astrid again. At least we won.

Tonight's game was against Vancouver, and we held them to two unanswered goals into the third period, and they were pissed. One of their D-men, a fucking goon if you ask me, body checked me into the boards in a dirty hit that took me out of the game. A set of X-rays later and luckily, no broken ribs. But one hell of a bruise. I'm questionable to return for our game in Detroit the day after tomorrow.

I convinced the trainers that I was okay enough not to be monitored overnight by one of the team's medical staff. Sort of regret that decision now, though. I'm sore as fuck and I could use someone here to just bring me things so I wouldn't have to move around the hotel room as much.

No sooner am I settled than a knock at the door forces me to hoist myself up off the couch. I swing open to door to see Justin's stupid face.

"Brought you some ice, man." He holds up a bag of ice from the ice machine.

"Thanks. I appreciate it." I take the bag from him.

"You gonna hang here or come down to the bar?"

"Nah, I'm just going to get some rest."

"Sounds good." He starts off down the hallway and calls over his shoulder, "Get yourself right. We're going to need you in Detroit."

"I'll do my best," I say as I swing the door shut.

I settle back down on the couch, wincing as I get the makeshift ice pack adjusted. This fucking blows. The more this season goes on, the more I'm beginning to think it might be my last.

This is the last year of my contract, and while I have no plans to leave Boston or entertain the idea of free agency, our owner has let me know in no uncertain terms that he plans on re-signing me, I just have to name my price. But my body isn't what it used to be. For twenty-nine, I might as well be fifty with as beat up and worn out as my joints are. Unlike a lot of aging athletes, I'm not under any illusions that my time on the ice is infinite.

After Astrid and my conversation yesterday at the Public Garden, I've been thinking more and more about what retirement might look like for me. I've always wanted to give back to kids whose parents struggled to pay for their training, and I'd love to finally have more time than just the offseason to do that. I'd have time to spoil Astrid the way she deserves to be spoiled. We could build a life together, a family. The image of Astrid with a baby bump brings a smile to my face. Maybe one day.

My ringing phone pulls me from my thoughts. Smiling when I see who it is, I answer.

"Hi, gorgeous."

"Hey." Astrid's warm, honeyed voice soothes my aching body.

"You're still up? I thought you would for sure be in bed by now." It's almost midnight here, and Boston is three hours ahead of us.

"I tried, but I couldn't sleep. I figured you would be out with the guys after the game, but I wanted to make sure you were okay after that hit."

I can hear how tired she is, and I love that she wanted to check on me. "I'm alright. Nothing a little rest won't fix."

"So, nothing's broken then? On the broadcast they said you were being taken back for X-rays, but then they never gave an update."

"No, nothing's broken. Just going to have a gnarly bruise in the morning."

"Are you going to be benched for the game in Detroit?" she asks.

"Nah. The biggest thing they were concerned about were broken ribs and beyond that, a bruise won't keep me out of the game."

I hear her take a massive yawn.

"I wish I was with you right now." I say, too tired and sore to care if it sounds needy.

"Well, I hate to tell you this, but I'm in bed with another man."

The fuck? "Astrid, what are you talk—"

"Yeah, he's about five feet tall, brown, really hairy, and very cuddly." I can hear her smile through the phone.

"Are you sleeping with that teddy bear you won on our date?"

"I am." She lets out a sleepy giggle. "I'm pretending it's you."

I chuckle, even though it hurts. "You should try to get some sleep. I know you've got that big ad campaign pitch in the morning." If I weren't so sore, I might try to talk her into having phone sex. On second thought, maybe not, the teddy bear would make it weird.

"Mmkay," she mumbles, clearly exhausted. "I love you."

"Love you too, baby. Sweet dreams."

"Night," she murmurs.

I wait to hear the call disconnect before I drop my phone onto the couch beside me. Wincing again, I haul my ass up, turn off all the lights, and crawl into a cold bed. As I drift off to sleep, I think about what my life could look like in a year. If I'm done with hockey or if I'm still playing, either way, Astrid will be in my bed. Of that, I'm sure.

***

I wake up at five in the morning to the sound of a blaring alarm clock and wince when I roll over. Just my body weight on my side causes a searing pain to radiate through me. *Shit.* Maybe I do need to sit out the game tomorrow. The trainers should at least reevaluate me.

As I pass by the full-length mirror, I do a double take at my reflection. A deep purple bruise covers my side from my armpit to my waist.

"Jesus," I say to myself. "That'll do it."

I haven't been bruised like this since college, when the coaches heavily implied that they approved of dirty hits without outright endorsing them. I snap a picture and send it to Astrid. She must be on the train on her way to work because she responds almost immediately.

Astrid: OH MY GOD!
Astrid: Are you sure you can play tomorrow???
Astrid: That's really bad

I laugh to myself at her rapid-fire texts. It's a very Astrid way to text. I type out a quick reply before throwing my things in my bag and heading out to the lobby to catch the team bus to the airport.

It's not typical that we travel this early after a game, but our schedule the week of Thanksgiving is always thrown off by the holiday. Add to it the fact that our organization teamed up with Detroit for a charity event tonight ahead of our game tomorrow.

I'm in a daze by the time we get to the plane, and I'm fast asleep before we even take off.

***

I take another nap when we get to the hotel in Detroit. It's astonishing how tired a little bruising can make you. When I wake up, I'm noticeably less sore than I was first thing this morning, so at least I've got that going for me.

I shower and get ready for our charity event. I usually enjoy being out in public for fundraisers, especially when we get to meet kids. They're always such big fans and the parents are always so appreciative of the time we spend with their kids, but the possibility of my stalker showing up tonight has me on edge.

During the event, I constantly look over my shoulder and scan the crowd. It's pathetic how much of a hold this stranger has on my life. I guess she's not strictly a stranger. She just couldn't handle being a one-night stand, even though she assured me she could. That's mostly why I hadn't hooked up with anyone in so long. Not until I met Astrid, at least.

Thinking about Astrid and how much I wish she was here makes my mood drop even lower. With the stalker being at the forefront of my mind since landing in Detroit, I haven't found a chance to call Astrid. Luckily, it's nearing the end of the event and I make an excuse to skip drinks with the guys at the bar. I'll have a chance to call her back at the hotel.

When I finally make it back to my hotel room, I strip out of my suit and fall onto the mattress. I'm asleep before I can even text Astrid.

***

My alarm goes off at eight the next morning and I open my eyes, confused about where I am until after a few blinks and scanning the room has shaken off the drowsiness.

I pick up my phone to see a missed call from Astrid. I call her back but get her voicemail. Instead of leaving her a message, I shoot her a quick text.

Me: Morning, baby. Sorry I didn't call you last night, I fell asleep as soon as I got back to the hotel. Hope you have a good day at work

I see the bubbles of her typing out a reply pop up instantly.

Astrid: Hey!
Astrid: No worries!
Astrid: Headed into a team meeting, otherwise would have picked up your call a second ago
Astrid: It's gonna be a busy day for me, I'll try to connect with you after your game
Astrid: Love you!

Her texts make me smile as they pop up. I type out a quick reply before heading down to the meeting room for the team's game-day catering.

When I get back up to my room, I jump in the shower before it's time to go to the arena for our morning skate.

The glass walls of the shower remind me of my shower at home, which reminds me of showering with Astrid. Before long, my dick is getting hard as my thoughts conjure up the image of Astrid, naked, wet, and begging me to fuck her. Leaning against one wall, I rest my forehead on my left forearm and palm my raging boner. Closing my eyes, I imagine it's Astrid stroking my cock and not my own right hand.

A knock at the door makes me pause for a moment. I listen, waiting for another knock, but when I don't hear one after a few seconds, I go back to thinking about Astrid.

This time, I imagine her pretty little lips wrapped around my cock as she takes me deep into the back of her throat. The memory of how it felt to have her choking on my cock and how sweet her pussy tastes has me about to come in no time. My ab muscles seize, and my balls constrict as I blow my load all over the shower wall.

My eyes shoot open as another noise from outside the bathroom grabs my attention. I know I heard that. It sounded like the room door slamming closed.

I turn off the shower and listen, but only hear silence and the drips of the water falling off the showerhead. I resume my shower, convincing myself that it was only the neighbor's door and I'm being a wimp. The other possibility, and the more likely one, is that Justin's fucking with me, knowing how jumpy I am anytime we're in the Midwest.

When I get down to the lobby to meet up with the rest of the team, I'm back to looking over my shoulder and scanning the crowd.

"Dude." Justin eyes me with concern. "You good? You look like shit."

I glare at him. "Thanks, asshole. I'm fine."

"You sure?" The look on his face shows genuine concern. Maybe it wasn't him at my door.

"Did you come by my room after breakfast?"

His brow knits together. "No, why?"

I shake my head. "Nothing, forget I said anything."

The team doctors insist on checking me out before I can join the team on the ice for practice. They clear me not five minutes after I go into the training exam room, and then I'm throwing on my equipment and speeding down the chute to the ice.

Being on the ice brings me clarity. I'm sure that I was being paranoid earlier. The exhilaration of running drills and new plays has me feeling renewed. Thank fuck, I feel like I can focus on the game now.

After practice, the team has a pre-game meal set up for us in one of the multipurpose rooms in the arena. We'll hang out in here until it's time to get suited up for the game in a few hours. We watch game tape and listen to the coaches go over the game plan for the night. The familiarity of it all calms the rest of my nervous energy. I haven't heard from Astrid at all, but she said she'd be busy. By the time we're standing on the ice listening to the national anthem being sung by a local blues singer, I'm back to feeling like myself.

The game itself is a shutout. We score three unanswered goals against Detroit in the first two periods. When they hit the ice for the third, they're pissed. The last period is honestly the first time the game has felt competitive.

"Nice of you to finally show up to the game." Justin taunts the other wing after they score their first goal of the night.

"I was too busy fucking Grant's girl." Their second-string center spits back as we get set for the faceoff.

The ref drops the puck, and I don't even go for it. Instead, I throw my gloves down and swing for this asshole's jaw before he can get away with the puck. The referee pulls me off him, but not until I get in a couple more good hits, and he smirks at me as he skates off the ice with a busted lip. They got what they wanted. A forced major penalty and a huge power play opportunity. And what do I get? Five minutes to sit in the sin bin and think about what it means to be "sportsmanlike."

How does that fucker even know about Astrid? It's not like our relationship is public knowledge. Not that we're keeping it private, but it's not even been something that's come up in interviews yet. It usually takes the media longer than a few weeks to catch on to developing relationships unless the couple puts it out there on social media.

By the time I'm zooming back on the ice, the sinking feeling has returned. Detroit managed to score a goal during their power play, but we hold our lead through to the last buzzer.

After everyone has showered, done media interviews, and is loaded up onto the bus to go back to the hotel, I finally turn my phone back on. Justin plops down in the seat next to me as a text pops up from an unknown number.

Unknown: YOU'RE A PIECE OF SHIT GRANT! WHAT DO YOU HAVE A GIRL IN EVERY FUCKING CITY??

Unknown: HOW COULD YOU DO THIS TO ASTRID KNOWING HER PAST AND WHAT SHE'S BEEN THROUGH

"Oh shit," I mutter under my breath.

Justin looks at me, then leans in to read over my shoulder.

"Oh shit," he echoes. "Who is that?"

"I don't know. Astrid's friend, Bailey maybe?" I spitball.

I rack my brain trying to figure out what the hell could have happened when another notification pops up, this time from Instagram saying I've been tagged in a post.

When the post loads, my heart feels like it fell out of my chest and rolled onto the floor of the bus. My fucking stalker. The picture is a selfie taken in the doorway of a hotel bathroom. A woman stands with her back to the rest of the bathroom. She's winking and sticking her tongue out. Over her shoulder is a clear shot of a man in the shower, leaning forward with his head resting on the forearm closest to the glass shower wall. An unmistakable purple bruise covers his left side.

26

Astrid

I should have known better than to rush into a new relationship with someone who is in a different city every day, six months out of the year. I feel so stupid. Of course he had side pieces. He had given me all the signs, the same ones I saw with Landon. But again, I ignored them. He was too charming, and I was too in love to see what was right in front of me. *Again.*

I saw the picture on Wednesday at lunch. They must have spent the night together Tuesday. I'm assuming that's the real reason he didn't call.

Because she's amazing and one of the few people who could never let me down, Bailey covered for me for the rest of Wednesday afternoon, and I went home to cry and wallow in my self-pity. I stayed up half the night crying, in fact. I cried until I thought I ran out of tears. Then I saw the teddy bear sitting in the corner of my bedroom and I started crying all over.

He's called and texted, and I have ignored every effort on his part to make contact. I glance at the clock. It's noon. I should be getting ready to go to Friendsgiving with the girls right now, but I can't bring myself to get out of bed. I can't bear the thought of sitting round the Thanksgiving table and saying what I'm grateful for. It would definitely kill everyone's turkey buzz.

I pull the covers up over my head. I'm a solid twenty-four hours into this, and I don't even feel like I've landed at the bottom of my pit of despair yet. Jesus, I sound so dramatic. I wasn't this upset after I found Landon balls deep in his coworker in *our* bed after being together for over *five years*. Why the *fuck* am I this torn up about a relationship that lasted less than a *month*?

My phone buzzes, and my arm shoots out from under the blankets. Like the pathetic little girl I am, I'm still hoping it's Cam.

Bailey: Do not cancel on me on Thanksgiving because of a DUDE
Bailey: Come hang out with us. We can drink wine and talk shit about men... or we could make you an account on Tinder

Groaning, I put my phone face down on my nightstand. I know if I leave her on read, she'll just call me until I answer. Right on cue, my phone buzzes with an incoming call.

"What?" I grumble after answering.

"Um, hi sis. Are you okay?" My oldest sister's voice is etched with concern and annoyance.

My brow furrows and I look at my phone screen for confirmation. Shit. Amber. Not Bailey. Now I'm going to have to explain what crawled up my ass and died on Thanksgiving. And she'll probably do me the favor of telling Mom and I'll have another phone call to look forward to later from her.

"Amber. I'm so sorry. I thought you were Bailey."

"Why are you so pissed off at Bailey?"

"I'm not."

"Sure did sound like it based on the way you answered the phone."

I close my eyes and force myself to take a deep breath. "I'm not upset with her. I just don't want to go and be social right now, and she's pressuring me is all."

"I see." She puts on her eldest-daughter voice. The one that commands as much authority over my brother and me as our mother's. "And why is it that you don't feel like spending Thanksgiving with neither your family nor your best friend?"

I huff out a breath, knowing that I won't get out of this. "I was seeing a guy who ended up also seeing someone else." Reducing my relationship with Cameron down to a single sentence has the tears pricking my eyes again.

"How long were you seeing this guy?"

"Like three weeks." It sounds so pathetic when I say it out loud.

"Oh, so you love him," she says bluntly.

"What? No—"

"Bullshit, Astrid. You don't think I remember having this same conversation with you after things ended with Landon? You may not agree with this, but you never truly loved Landon. He was convenient for you."

I scoff. "Wow. Thanks for the pep talk, sis."

"I'm sorry, but this is the reality you face when you open up and give your heart to someone. That's not to say you should stop doing it, either." Commotion in the background comes through the phone. It sounds like utter chaos over there. "I gotta go, Mom just spilled the entire pot of sweet potatoes. Probably on purpose, too."

I laugh. Our mom hates sweet potatoes. My siblings and I are indifferent to them, but our dad loved them. Sweet potatoes were his favorite part of Thanksgiving. My mom still makes them every year in his honor.

Amber continues, "You're going to get through this, I promise."

I smile. "Thanks sis."

As soon as I set my phone down, it rings again. This time, it *is* Bailey.

I roll my eyes. "Bailey, I'm not coming." Despite the talk with my sister, I just don't want to be around people right now.

"Come on," Bailey whines.

"No."

"Astrid, I know how much you cared about him and how you must feel—"

My frustration bubbles to the surface, and I cut her off. "But you don't know how I feel, Bailey. All you ever do is hook up. You've never had a connection with someone like I did with—"

My outburst dies on a sob.

Bailey takes a deep breath and blows it out slowly.

"Astrid," she says calmly, "I love you. I'm going to give you the space you clearly need right now. I will be there when you want someone, you just let me know when that is."

"Bailey, I'm sorry—"

"I know. You don't have to apologize, I pushed you. It's okay. I love you, girl."

I say goodbye and hang up, feeling way worse than I did a minute before. Bailey doesn't deserve my anger. She's been my best friend for as long as I've known her. She's a goddamn saint for as much grace as she just showed me.

I shuffle between my bed and the couch the rest of the weekend. Sunday afternoon, I catch a glimpse of myself in the bathroom mirror. My hair is a greasy rat's nest, and my eyes are puffy from all the crying I've been doing. I walk back out to the living room and take in my surroundings. Takeout containers litter the entire kitchen and living room. And there's a weird smell that I'm not convinced isn't me.

Sighing, I head back to the bathroom for a long-overdue shower. I'll let the water rinse away the rest of my sadness.

***

I walk into work Monday morning with my head held high. I'm not sure if word has spread around the office yet that my heart got broken, but I'd rather spare myself the awful sympathy pouts people gave me after I ended things with Landon. I didn't need the sympathy then, and I sure as *fuck* don't need it now.

I open my email to an onslaught of unread messages from clients. I swear some people never take a damn day off, and they're surprised that anyone else would either.

Bailey waltzes into my office with two cups of coffee and a brown paper bag from my favorite donut shop in Beacon Hill. She sets the bag and one cup down on my desk and I eye them suspiciously.

"Is that a sympathy donut? Because if it is, I don't want it."

She smiles at me. "It's a good thing it's not, then."

I take a sip of the latte. "I'm sorry," I say softly.

She waves me off. "Don't be. I'm just glad you're done with being a sad bitch and back to being a bad bitch like me. It's been rough out here without you."

I laugh. "Love you, B."

She starts to walk out of my office, then turns around. "Oh, I know you probably don't feel like doing this, but we're going out tonight."

I raise my eyebrows. "And why would I not feel like doing that, exactly?"

A shit-eating grin spreads across her face. "Exactly." She struts out of my office.

After work, Bailey and I head to a bar to drink. We walk inside and realize that the place is more of a sports bar than the Irish pub it's advertised to be.

"Let's go find someplace else." Bailey tugs at my elbow.

"Why would we need to? There's no reason we can't drink here." I almost convince myself.

We find a table near the back and order drinks and a few appetizers.

"So"—Bailey pokes at my arm— "have you returned any of his calls yet?"

I shake my head while the waitress sets down our drinks. "Why bother? It's not like our relationship meant enough for him to *not* sleep around."

I look up at her, expecting her to have a witty retort ready, but instead, she's silent, her eyes fixed on the TV behind me. I turn around and see none other than *the* Cameron. Fucking. Grant.

Fuck. In all my self-pity, I forgot they were playing at home tonight. It's too loud in the bar to hear the broadcast, but from the captions on the screen, I surmise that there's been some very aggressive play by Boston tonight.

As much as I hate myself for doing it, I find myself watching him, all fire and hatred, as he slams one of St.

Louis's players into the boards and starts pummeling him with his fists. Out of nowhere, several more players from each team are on them, and I can't tell if they're trying to pull them apart or throw more punches.

"Oh my God," Bailey gasps behind me, but my eyes are glued to the screen as the fight finally gets broken up.

The camera zooms in on Cameron as he's escorted off the ice. He has a split lip and one of his eyes is already puffy, with what is sure to be a black eye. My heart clinches at the sight of him hurt. I still love him, but I remind myself that this hurt that I'm feeling right now, while temporary, will only repeat itself if I go back to him. And that is something I refuse to do.

Turning back around in my seat, I nibble on the appetizers the waitress drops off for us. I don't have much of an appetite, and my thoughts drift back to Cameron. I keep going over all our time together, looking for any indication that he would hurt me, but I struggle to come up with anything.

Landon made being in a relationship with him look like a red flag factory. But when you're in love, or what you think is love, you see everything through rose-colored glasses. When those glasses are in place, all the warning signs just look like regular flags.

When the rose-colored glasses came off with Landon, I finally realized how messed up our relationship was. It was like when we were together, there were a thousand puzzle pieces I couldn't sort through, but after the breakup, all those pieces fell into place and I could finally see the full picture. I could finally see all the manipulation and ulterior motives of his actions.

With Cameron, even with the benefit of hindsight, I'm still left staring at a jumbled pile of puzzle pieces with no idea what I'm supposed to be looking at. His actions all seemed, and still seem, genuine. He even sat there and looked pissed when I told him about the shitty ways Landon had treated me. I just can't seem to reconcile that with the fact that he has another girlfriend in Detroit.

I guess I really shouldn't compare my relationship with Landon to my relationship with Cameron. First, they lasted dramatically different amounts of time. Second, I never felt the way for Landon as I did, or still do, for Cameron. Or maybe I'm still wearing those rose-colored glasses.

Fuck me. I feel the sting of new tears burning the backs of my eyes and I lean forward with a groan, propping my elbows on the table and burying my face in my hands.

Bailey's hand rubs up and down my upper arm. "It'll be okay, sweetie. I promise."

Her words of encouragement do nothing for my public display of heartbreak and, as much as I try to fight them off, the tears break free.

Without saying a word, Bailey uses the tablet at our table and swipes her card to pay our bill, and we leave without finishing either our drinks or food.

We load up into an Uber together and head to my apartment.

“We can stop by your place first.” I say, wiping my eyes. “You don’t have to ride all the way up to Somerville, only to ride all the way back down to Back Bay.”

“It’s okay, I don’t mind.” She grabs my hand, and we ride the rest of the way in silence.

27

Cameron

I got thrown out of my fucking game. Still worked up over what that asshole defenseman from St Louis said, I throw my helmet across the locker room and slump down on the bench in front of my locker. I've never been kicked out of a game over misconduct before. It's my own fault, just like this whole fucked-up situation with Astrid.

Last week, when the team arrived back at the hotel after our game in Detroit, I marched right up to the manager and let out all my rage at him for the incompetence of his staff. My stalker conned the front desk staff into believing that she was my assistant and had gear to drop off for me. They happily handed her the key to my fucking room, despite being told to be on the lookout for someone matching her description.

Detective Mathis *finally* had clear evidence she violated the restraining order and was able to arrest her. I thought that would be the end of the whole ordeal, but then the fucking media sunk their claws into the story. The local Detroit news circuit broke the story, no doubt their source being from the hotel staff, given the explicit details they ran. The story then got picked up by ESPN and SportsCenter, who showed a heavily blurred out version of the picture she posted alongside her mug shot.

Not only has this psycho ass stalker ruined the one meaningful relationship I've had in my adult life, but her actions have also forced me to face the hardest decision I never thought I'd have to: either leave Boston to play for another team or retire. The Bears organization does not tolerate lewd behavior. When the owner caught wind that one of his players had a naked photo circulating the internet, he was calling for blood. After the head coach and general manager went to bat for me, explaining the whole situation, he backed down on the suspension. But that whole "name your price" deal he gave me for next season? It's off the table now. Zero chance I'll be playing in Boston next year.

I want to be mad and blame everyone, but I know it's my fault. If only I had told her what was going on. I could have warned her something might happen. I could have told her not to believe anything that might be posted by that delusional woman who thinks we're in love. What good would that have done? The picture was pretty damning, and now there's the possibility that I won't have a future with either hockey or Astrid.

I've tried calling and texting Astrid nearly three dozen times in the five days since that damn picture dropped and broke the internet. Every single one has gone unanswered. I thought maybe she might see the news coverage and realize that it had all been a big misunderstanding. But I understand what she must be thinking of me right now, and if space is what she needs, then that's what I'll give her. I only hope her need for space is temporary and she'll come back to me.

As the rest of the team files in to the locker room after the game, I decide I need to pay Astrid a visit at her office. Justin plops down next to me at his locker.

"You okay?" he asks.

"I'll be fine. Just a busted lip is all," I reply coldly.

"I'm not talking about the busted lip, man." He fixes me with a look.

I nod and look down at the floor. "I'm going to go see her tomorrow when she gets off work."

"She gonna actually hear what you have to say?"

"Fuck if I know."

***

I sit in the lobby of Astrid's office building thinking about the last time I was here waiting for her. That was only a few weeks ago and, since that moment, we fell in love, talked about a future together, and then had it all come crashing down around us.

The elevator chimes and I stand, praying Astrid is somewhere in the crowd of people that come pouring out into the lobby. I scan the group but don't see her. Disappointed, I sit back down until the next chime announces the arrival of more people. Searching this crowd of people turns up no Astrid, but one familiar face comes barreling toward me.

Bailey must be all of five feet tall in three-inch heels, but the look on her face and the fury radiating out of her petite frame would make even the toughest guys in the NHL do whatever she told them.

"Grant." She sneers.

"Hi, Bailey." I swallow over the gravel in my throat. I've never seen a woman this small this furious before. "I'm just here to apologize and speak to Astrid."

"Do you remember our deal?" she clips.

"Our deal?" The realization dawns a second later. "Oh no way, you can't be—"

Before I can even brace myself, her knee connects directly to my balls. I double over in pain and hear the clicks of her heels as she marches back toward the doors onto Clarendon Street. I glance up, trying to catch my breath, and my eyes land on Astrid. This may be my moment to finally explain myself. But as Bailey approaches her, Astrid turns her back to me and walks right out the door with her best friend at her side.

And that right there, that look on Astrid's face like she doesn't even know me, hurts way worse than the knee to my balls.

28

Astrid

Turning around and walking away from Cameron was the hardest thing I've ever done. It took every ounce of courage and sheer force of will for me not to run into his arms. I refuse to be the girl who can be talked back into a relationship by someone who can so easily hurt me. I may have been that girl a year ago, but not anymore.

It's been a week since he showed up in the lobby of my office building. A week of nightly phone calls and text messages that are getting more and more difficult to ignore. I should block his number, but I can't bring myself to do it. The most frustrating thing about it is he probably knows that and that's why he keeps calling.

I hit play on the latest voicemail and his warm voice makes me wish he was here.

"Astrid. It's me again. Please call me back, baby. I know by now you've seen the news story, and you know the truth so why are you still ignoring me? Put me out of my misery here. I can't take this. Please call me back."

Guilt washes over me. It's wrong of me to not give him any answers. I'm just worried that if I agree to meet with him in person, my body will betray me and I'll end up giving in to temptation. No. I need to do this over the phone. He needs, and deserves, an explanation for my continued silence.

I check the Bears schedule. As luck would have it, they are playing an away game tonight. Good. If I call him, there's no chance of him demanding we do this face to face.

I dial his number and he picks up on the first ring.

"Astrid, I'm so relieved you called me b—"

I cut him off. "Cameron, I have a lot to say, and I think it's best if you just listen and let me get it all out."

I hear him sucking in a breath over the line. "Sure, yeah. I can listen."

I blow out a breath, bracing myself. Better to just rip the band aid off. "First, I want to apologize to you for not reaching out soon—"

"Baby, you have nothing to be so—"

I cut him right back off. "Cameron, just let me talk. Please." The last word comes out barely above a whisper, the tears threatening to make an appearance already. I take a deep breath and continue. "I should have reached out sooner. It wasn't fair to keep you hanging, so for that I'm sorry."

I pause. Waiting for him to interrupt me again. When he doesn't, I continue.

"Second, my waiting to reach out has nothing to do with your stalker. At first it did, but it only took a few days before I was ready to watch the news and realized it was a misunderstanding."

A huge ball of hot bile threatens to come up from my stomach just thinking about what I'm about to say.

"The reason I've been ignoring your calls and texts is because I can't be in a relationship. I rushed into this when I should have just spent more time figuring out who I am as a single woman before getting back into a relationship. I need to take the time for myself to do that. I'm so sorry that it took something like this stalker incident to make me realize it. I wish I had been able to recognize it sooner and put an end to things, I just—" The end of that sentence gets lost on a sob and I hold my breath a moment, trying to calm myself. I refuse to let him know that I'm hurting right now. It will only make things harder for the both of us.

He blows out a puff of air. "I understand. I'll give you whatever space you need to figure things out, and for as long as it takes. You just let me know when you're ready."

The tears spill out from behind my eyes. "Cameron, I can't have you waiting in the wings for me. I can't be the reason that you're not out there living your life and meeting people and trying to find the person you want to build your life with."

He laughs at that. "Astrid, I've already met that person. Regardless of when, or if, you decide you're ready to get back out there, this is it for me. I can tell you with a hundred percent certainty, there is no one else on this planet that I would even consider building a life with. I hope that one day you change your mind about me, but if you don't, that's okay too. I want you to be happy. If that's with me, great. But if it's not, then I want you to find the person who can give you the life you want and deserve."

"You can't do that. I can't do what I need to do and be by myself if I think you're out there waiting for me to come back to you."

He laughs again. "Astrid, you and I both know neither one of us can control how we feel. Don't worry about me, I'll be okay."

Tears pour freely from my eyes, and I draw in a shaky breath. "Goodbye, Cameron."

"Bye, Astrid."

I hang up and let the sobs overtake me, my body shuddering violently. This is what I wanted. So why does it feel like I just ripped out my own heart and smashed it into a million pieces?

***

The following night, Bailey and I decide to have a quiet girls' night in after work. We take an Uber from the office to my place and order Thai for dinner.

We sit on the floor and watch a cheesy holiday romance movie about a woman who constantly focuses on her career, then realizes what a jerk her big-time corporate boyfriend is when her flight from New York to Los Angeles gets diverted to a small-town airport due to a snowstorm. She falls in love with the local small-town hottie.

"I don't understand why they didn't just cancel the flight," Bailey says, getting up to raid my freezer for ice cream after we're done with our Thai.

"Because then there wouldn't be a movie," I laugh.

This is the first night that things have felt somewhat normal. I feel like I can breathe again. At least a little.

Bailey comes back into the living room with her ice cream and something small in her hand. She holds it out to me.

"Why do you still have this up, Astrid?" she asks, her tone laced with pity.

I look up and my eyes land on the Polaroid that the creepy college student snapped of Cameron and me at the suspension bridge in the Public Garden. The photo was snapped right after Cameron set me on my feet and took my face in his hands. The look of love shared between us jumps out of the picture. It's hard for me to look at but, honestly, I also love it. I should get rid of it or put it away somewhere, but I can't bring myself to do it.

Before I can answer, she just laughs and shakes her head, plopping down on the couch next to me.

"Why are you laughing?"

"Because you're lying to yourself if you honestly think you can just walk away from that man," she says.

"Bailey, you know I rushed into it. I need to be by myself and learn what it means for me to be single. I thought you, of all people, would understand that."

She rolls her eyes. "Bullshit, Astrid. You think any single person out there legitimately *wants* to be single the rest of their lives? That they don't *want* to find someone to spend their life with. I can tell you from experience"—she holds up the picture again—"this right here, is the look I would fucking die to have just once. And you insist you don't want it. I don't believe you for a second when you say you *want* to be single."

"Bailey, I—"

"Just answer me one question."

I blow out the rest of the air in my lungs and close my eyes. "Okay."

"Are you using this breakup as a way to avoid being vulnerable with Cameron?"

Her question hits me like a punch to the gut.

She rolls her eyes again. "Come on, girl. I've known you for way too long for you to bullshit me now."

We both laugh, breaking the tension.

She continues. "For real, look at the facts. You were with Landon for *years*. Your whole life fell apart when you found out he was cheating on you. You lost your home, your financial security, your partner, your future. You had to totally rebuild your life, and you didn't miss one fucking step along that path. And you were such a badass to watch. Now..." She grasps my hand. "Now, I see you hurting over a relationship that lasted a fraction of that time and I don't know what to do to get my badass bestie back."

I snicker. "Since when are you such a ballbuster?"

She laughs and reaches for her coat on the back of one of my dining area chairs. “You’re such a jerk. I’m gonna get out of here. Love you, bestie.”

I walk her to the door, and we say goodbye.

I really don’t know what I would do without my best friend. I think about what she said about whether I’m using this breakup to avoid being vulnerable and opening myself up to hurt. Ultimately, it doesn't matter. I *was* vulnerable and I *did* get hurt. If anything, it made me realize I can’t let one person’s presence in my life dictate my happiness.

29

Cameron

In the two weeks since Astrid said she needed space, I've done my best to give her just that. Physical space, at least. I've spent countless hours scrolling her social media for a glimpse of what she's been doing. Which, from the looks of it, isn't much.

I'm on day one of two back-to-back days off between home games. Normally, I would be doing extra training sessions on my own, but lately, if it's not required, I haven't been super motivated to do it. Despite my ambivalence toward going above and beyond our team's regular practice schedule, my head and heart are back in the game itself. And as a team, we're working so well together that we're at the top of the entire league.

A text pops up over top of a post Astrid made months ago, partially blocking her face from my view.

I click on the notification and frown at the screen. It's my business partner and chef from Danza Lento.

Maurice: Hey Cam, I need you to come in today to go over

marketing materials for Valentine's Day

Valentine's Day? It's only the week of Christmas. And since when does he put together a marketing strategy? We've been booked solid since we opened, with a wait list a mile long. We don't need to advertise.

Me: Is marketing necessary? We're booked solid until May

Maurice: Yes. And I need you to come down here now. I've been trying to get you to sign off on these for weeks now.

He has? I have no recollection of any of this. Why does he need me to sign off on anything? That's the point of me being a *silent* partner. I just bankroll whatever he needs.

Groaning, I type out a reply.

Me: Be there in ten

I order an Uber on my way down to the lobby. It's too cold to walk the mile to the restaurant from my condo, and it will take longer to wait on my SUV from the valet than it will to drive over there, never mind the time it'll take to park.

I stride into the restaurant at the height of lunch rush. Normally, I use the door off the back alley during business hours, so I don't disrupt any guests, but today I just didn't care. I scan the dining room quickly as I pass by the hostess stand, but before I get very far past it, I hear the lilting laugh of the woman who holds my heart.

I stop dead in my tracks, and my head snaps in the direction of her laugh. She's here. She's facing away from me and my heart drops when I see a man sitting with her, laughing at whatever she just said. I approach her from behind, and the eyes of the man she's sitting with meet mine.

"Oh shit," he says, his smile gone and eyes wide as he looks up at me.

She turns in her chair, and when her eyes meet mine, I swear all the air gets sucked out of the dining room.

"Cameron," she says softly. "This—"

"You're here with Tyler?" The hurt is evident in my voice. The woman who broke both our hearts because she needed to be single is here on a fucking date? With the guy who got so drunk at a bar that he didn't object to the suggestion he leave without her, leaving her there alone with twenty other guys and no way to get home? Fury coils around my spine.

"It's not a date," she says quickly. "We're here because of work. We both landed big accounts this quarter, and the firm rewarded us with lunch here."

Her explanation does little to reduce the hurt and anger I'm sure are obvious in the way I'm standing and staring down at the two of them. A quick glance around the dining room tells me I've already caused more of a scene than necessary.

"Well, you two enjoy the rest of your meal. I hear the tiramisu is delicious."

I turn and walk straight back out the front door, not bothering to stop and check with Maurice. I'll get it sorted out with him later. Right now, I just need to put as much space between myself and Astrid as possible.

***

I was beyond hurt and angry when I got home yesterday, but I finally decided that there's still something that Astrid isn't telling me. I spent the rest of the day poring over everything she ever told me, searching for something that might shed some light on why she would be so willing to put herself through this. She must not be telling me everything. I suspect it's something she's not even able to admit to herself. But how can I get her to agree to talk to me?

I look out of the massive windows in my living room. Snow has been falling all morning in what is turning out to be the first real snow of the season. I know Astrid is out there, probably at work, watching the snow fall as well. I know I told her I would be waiting for her if or when she was ready for a relationship, but I can't wait anymore. Every day she's out there is another day I'm missing out on all the things that make my life worth living. Her smile, her laugh, the feel of her in my arms. I need her like I need air and without her, I'm fucking drowning.

I groan and close my eyes, willing the universe to give me a plan when my phone lights up with an incoming call from the concierge downstairs.

"Hello?" I answer.

"Good afternoon, Mr. Grant. I have a guest down here who is insisting on seeing you."

That's weird. If it were one of the guys from the team, or even Astrid for that matter, they would just key in the code and come right up to my penthouse without bothering to check in at the concierge. It can't be anyone I know. And if it's no one I know, then nothing good will come of me inviting them up to my condo.

"No, please send them away. I'm not in the mood for visitors."

I listen to the concierge tell them I'm not taking visitors at the moment. It sounds like whoever is there isn't taking no for an answer, they argue, and then a crackling sound comes through the line.

"Cameron, it's Bailey. I need to talk to you. Let me up."

"Bailey? Is everything okay?" Now I'm convinced nothing good will come of this.

"Dammit, Grant. Just let me up. I need to talk to you, and I don't want to do it using the concierge's phone."

I debate it for a second, then give her the code for my floor. Whatever her reason for showing up on my doorstep, it must be important enough for her to come see me in the middle of a workday.

I pace my kitchen while I wait for Bailey before deciding to open the door to my condo and stand out in the hall. The thought occurs to me that she might be here to kick me in the balls again. Shit. I ran into Astrid yesterday. Does she think I was stalking her? To her, it looks like I just walked into the restaurant, saw her, questioned whether or not she was on a date, then left after finding out it was a work thing. Should I put on a cup?

Too late. The elevator chimes, announcing Bailey's arrival. She steps off the elevator and approaches me slowly.

"Hey." She gives me a half smile.

"Hi, Bailey. Come on in." I relax a little bit. She's clearly not pissed off at me.

I let her walk past me into my condo. She pauses a moment just inside the door, waiting for me to show her which direction to go in the entry hall. When we round the corner into the open-concept kitchen, dining, and living rooms, she gasps.

"Wow, this place is amazing."

"Thanks. Can I take your coat?"

"I can't stay long."

"Alright then. Let's get down to it. Why are you here? I hope not to kick me in the balls again."

She winces. "I'm sorry about that."

I shrug. "It's okay. I kind of deserved it at the time."

She looks down and shifts her weight back and forth between her feet. I don't think I've ever seen her nervous before. It's highly unsettling. I motion to a barstool at the kitchen island, and she takes a seat while I walk around to face her from the other side, my back to the rest of the kitchen.

"Is everything okay?" I lean down onto the counter and prop myself up on my elbows.

She stares over my shoulder at something behind me.

"Bailey, is everything okay?" I repeat.

"What? Yeah, it's fine. Well, no. It's not, actually."

"Can you tell me what's wrong?"

She nods toward the fridge. "It's the picture."

"The picture?" I turn around and follow her gaze.

The picture from the suspension bridge that the creepy college kid snapped the moment I picked Astrid up and spun her around. My back is toward the camera, but it had a clear shot of Astrid's face. The look on it is one of pure joy. There's not just a trace of the real Astrid in the photo, it's one hundred percent the real Astrid, not some version she projects for someone else.

My brows knit together. "What wrong with it?"

"Well, nothing, it's just..." she hesitates. "Astrid has the same one. Well, not the exact same one but, from the same day."

I shrug. "Why is that an issue?"

She rolls her eyes. "Because you guys are clearly in love with each other."

My eyebrows shoot up and I scoff. "Yeah, well, Astrid has made it very clear that she's aware of that and wants to be single, anyway."

"Cameron, she's not happy."

"It's not my job to make her happy anymore. I tried and she doesn't want me."

"You know she's miserable, right? She pretends to be okay, but she's not."

I throw my hands up. "What am I supposed to do, Bailey? She wants me to leave her alone."

"No, she doesn't."

It's my turn to roll my eyes. I open my mouth to speak, but she puts up a hand to stop me.

"I've known Astrid since kindergarten. She has never been this upset over a breakup. Earlier this year, when her engagement ended, her entire world turned upside down. She didn't miss a fucking beat. I watched her be in that relationship for five years. I spent time with her and Landon together countless times." She points to the fridge. "That look on her face? I've never seen her look so happy. She may have said she wants to be left alone, but it's just an act. It's just her pretending she doesn't need anyone. She doesn't *want* to need anyone. But she *needs* you."

I blow out a slow breath and scrub my hand over the stubble forming on my chin. "What am I supposed to do?"

She chuckles. "Have you seen the snow? First real snow of the season."

30

Astrid

I close my eyes and take a deep breath, trying to shut out the world for just a minute longer. I've spent my lunch hour in the Public Garden watching the snow fall from the suspension bridge over the pond. The pond itself hasn't quite frozen over yet and reflects the snow-covered branches of the willow trees that encircle the pond.

Not many people travel outside during a snowstorm, but for me, it's my favorite time to be out in the city. The freshly fallen snow muffles the ambient city sounds, lending a rare, tranquility to the normally bustling city. I glance down at my phone to check the time. I have ten minutes before I need to start back toward the office. Slipping my phone back into the pocket of my coat, I catch some movement at the end of the bridge out of the corner of my eye.

Without looking, I know who it is. I look anyway. My stomach does a somersault when we lock eyes, just like it's always done and probably will continue to do until the end of time. I turn back to the pond as he starts toward me, closing my eyes and hoping it's just a ghost and he'll disappear. But he doesn't. He moves slowly, coming to a stop right beside me. Right where we once stood and talked about a life together. Our life. Our future.

He props his elbows on the railing and looks out over the pond. His closeness turns my legs to jelly, and it takes every ounce of my willpower not to close the remaining distance and let him wrap me up in his arms. I don't know why he's here or how he knew I'd be here. I can't put my thoughts into words to ask, either.

By the time he finally speaks, my heart feels like it's about to beat through my chest.

"Astrid—"

"I don't want your apology." It comes out way too aggressive and I wince. "We had an amazing time together, but it's over now. Let's just go our separate ways and call it a day. I can't be the girl whose whole life hinges on a single person." It kills me to push him away, but it's for the best. Right?

"I would never want that for you," he says sincerely. "I know that you're afraid to get hurt, but I also know you want to be with me."

I close my eyes and focus on my breathing, trying to come up with something that might sound convincing enough because my current line of reasoning, *I can't be with you because I want to be with you too much* won't cut it.

"Cameron, you know about my family's history. How my dad died hours after I was born. I grew up hearing stories from relatives and family friends about how much my parents loved each other, how sad it was that my mom could never bring herself to remarry because of that love.

The accident not only took my dad away from me, but it took my mom away from me, too. She was a hollowed-out shell after my dad died, and I grew up never really knowing either one of them. I promised myself a long time ago that I would never let the loss of someone be the death of me like it was for my mom."

He takes a step toward me, arm stretched out like he's about to touch my cheek. I step back, knowing that if I let him touch me, my resolve will break.

"Astrid," he says as he lets his arm fall to his side, "you can pull away from me all you want. It doesn't change anything for me. This is it for me. *You* are it for me. I can either spend the rest of my life beside you or love you from afar, but either way, I'm never going to stop loving you. And as much as you don't want to admit it, you feel the same way."

He takes another step, closing the gap between us and cups either side of my face. I'm too busy trying to fight back the tears that threaten to spill over to step out of his reach.

"You can't live your life as if it's already ended," he says. "If you do, then you've already died. I'd rather take the risk that one of us dies tomorrow, leaving the other one to feel this pain, if it gives us just one more night together."

I blink and the tears roll down my cheeks. Cameron swipes them away with his thumbs. He leans forward and rests his forehead on mine. I close my eyes and take another breath, inhaling his masculine scent.

"Don't do this to us, baby," he whispers. "Don't force us to both live as if we've already lost the most important thing in our lives. Don't make this decision for us both out of the fear of getting your heart broken, because the truth of it is, you're breaking your own heart if you do."

His breath ghosts over my lips as he says his last words, severing the thin shred of my resolve that remained. My heart is racing as I utter the word, "Okay."

Cameron's mouth collides with mine. His kiss is urgent, and his tongue dives into my mouth as I twist my fingers into his hair. Our kiss is like a balm to my aching soul. I didn't realize how exhausted I've been from trying to force myself to be okay with not being with him.

He pulls away just enough to look into my eyes. "Say it. Say you're done trying to fight this. Say you're mine."

"I'm yours," I say against his lips.

"I love you so much." He kisses me again.

I almost lose myself in the kiss this time. I'm ready to spend the rest of the day here, on this bridge, kissing him, but I pull back.

"I know this is really bad timing, but I have to get back to work," I tell him, so disappointed that I have to go.

He grins at me. "No, you don't."

My brow furrows. "I have work, I have to go. My lunch hour is over."

"You should check your phone."

I quirk up an eyebrow at him but do as he says. I have an unread text.

Bailey: Don't you even think about coming back to work. Whether or not you decide to be with him, just take the rest of the day. I'll cover for you.

I open my mouth to say something, but I have no words.

Cam snickers. "Bailey might have stopped by my condo earlier."

"You know," I say, "if it wasn't for Bailey, I probably wouldn't have ever spent the night with you in Vegas. Or gone on the date with Tyler that brought us back together."

"Can we please stop talking about Bailey? My balls still shrivel up inside me just thinking about her."

I laugh and bring my mouth close to his as I speak against his lips. "Maybe we should go back to your place so I can coax them out of hiding for you."

"Oh *fuck* yes."

31

Cameron

Six Weeks Later

The last few weeks with Astrid have been nothing short of amazing. We've spent every day together and every night, well, the same. We've fallen into such a comfortable and normal routine that makes it feel as if we've been together our whole lives. She's been an amazing support to me while I figure out what I'm going to do after this season, but right now, my focus is steering my team on to the playoffs.

I take that back. While my focus *is* on taking my team to the championship, it's *also* on spending the next six days in Aruba with Astrid. We're coming up to the midseason bye week, and I plan on keeping her locked away in our luxury suite at the all-inclusive resort. And we leave for paradise tomorrow. That is, of course, if the weather holds off for us to get out of Boston. There's a huge storm rolling in and they're calling for over eighteen inches of snow in the next twenty-four hours.

I've spent the last five days on the road with the team, and I am so ready to get home to Astrid. Home in the general sense, that is. Despite my best efforts to get her to move in with me, she wants to hold on to her own independence for a little while longer, which I'm fine with.

It's crazy to think that we've only been together for three months. I don't count the month that she lost her mind and tortured us both by deciding to be single. We don't talk about that. I've always heard people say "When you know, you know." That rings so true when it comes to my relationship with Astrid. I know I want to spend the rest of my life with her.

That's why, before the team left New York to go back to Boston ahead of our bye week, I had a very special box to pick up. Having the last game before our week off against New York gave me the perfect cover to pick up the custom engagement ring from Tiffany's.

I will admit, I did get some input from Bailey on what Astrid would like, but I had a solid idea of what I wanted to get her. I went with a one-carat cushion cut diamond solitaire. The diamond is the highest grade in color and is internally flawless. It might have cost a significant amount more to get the highest grade, but I will only ever give Astrid the best I possibly can.

As I walk into the lobby of my building, I see someone I don't expect.

"Hey, Jess. What are you doing here?"

"Cameron, hi. Sorry, I'm in a rush. I just emailed you details, but long story short, your flight out in the morning was cancelled. All flights for the next three days, actually. The whole airport is shut down. I just dropped off a week's worth of groceries for you since you're going to be stuck here instead of in paradise."

Disappointment floods me. Shit. I was going to propose on the beach at sunset. It was supposed to be perfect. "Okay, that sucks, but we'll manage. Thank you for thinking of me and getting groceries."

She starts off toward the door, walking backwards so she can continue talking to me. "No problem! I gotta run and get Justin his shit now. Good luck, by the way!" She winks, then turns around and scurries out the door.

On the elevator ride up to my condo, I try to see the positive side of things. If we get as much snow as they're calling for, Astrid and I will be locked up tight in my condo for at least the next seventy-two hours. That right there rivals Aruba for paradise in my book.

I walk into my condo and see Astrid putting away the groceries Jess just dropped off.

"Hey!" She grins at me and rounds the kitchen island.

I pull her into my arms and give her a quick kiss. I bury my face in her brunette waves and inhale the sweet scent of her shampoo. "Mmmm, I missed you."

She hums. "I missed you, too."

"So, I take it you were here when Jess came by?" I ask, releasing my grip on her.

"I was. Did you bump into her on her way out?"

"I did."

"Ahh. So, she told you about our flight?"

I heave a huge sigh of disappointment. "Yeah, she did. I'm so sorry, Astrid. I know how much you were looking forward to the trip."

She waves a hand in dismissal. "Don't be. I'd much rather be curled up on the couch here in front of your fireplace watching the snow than on a beach feeling the sweat drip down my boobs."

I laugh. "Okay, let me rephrase. I was really looking forward to the trip and seeing you in a bikini all week."

She snorts at that. "It's your lucky day then, because it just so happens that I brought my bikini with me."

I clutch my chest. "Baby. For me?"

She laughs again. I'm so happy I get to hear that sound for the rest of my life. Provided she says yes.

"Alright, I'm going to go shower. Then I want to see you in that bikini." I wink at her and leave her in the kitchen.

I would normally help her put away the groceries, but I need to stash the ring somewhere while Astrid is busy. I turn in circles around the bedroom, considering all the options that aren't places Astrid would typically look. As I'm looking around, I hear her coming down the hall toward the bedroom, so I quickly toss my unopened duffel into the closet and duck into the bathroom before she walks into the room.

She talks to me through the open bathroom door about her week at work while I shower. How the new client she has is a real piece of work, demanding she be on call twenty-four hours a day for whatever they need. Seriously, who needs advertising so urgently it can't wait until normal business hours?

When I get out of the shower and I'm all dried off, I walk into the bedroom. I thought Astrid had gone out to the living room since her side of the conversation had died down, so I'm surprised to see her sitting on the edge of the king-sized bed.

My stomach drops when I see my open duffel sitting next to her on the mattress. She's facing away from me, so I can't see what she's looking at, but when I round the corner of the bed, my suspicions are confirmed.

"Astrid..." My eyes land on the small blue box.

She blinks up at me and motions toward the open duffel. "I was going to throw your clothes in the laundry, but I..." She holds up the box, furrowing her brow. "What is this?"

I squat down in front of her. "I think you know what it is."

"I think I do, but I don't want to be disappointed so I'm hoping it's a pair of earrings." Tears well up in her eyes.

I smile. "It's not earrings." I gingerly take the box from her and swallow over the sand that coats my throat.

I take out the velvet ring box from the blue box and slowly open the lid. She sucks in a sharp breath as her eyes land on the enormous diamond ring. Taking out the ring, I hold her left hand in mine, the ring poised to slide into place on her finger.

"Astrid"—I look into her emerald-green eyes— "I know this is fast. There are a million things we have yet to encounter together and that we still need to figure out. But I don't want to wait until our ducks are in a row to ask you this."

"Cameron." She stops me. "Are you about to propose to me fully nude?"

My lips purse and I look down at my body. I had forgotten that I was naked. *It's okay, I can work with this*. "Will it change your answer if I say yes?"

"No."

"Will you marry me?"

"Yes, of course I will." Tears stream from her eyes, but her smile tells me they're out of sheer joy.

Standing, I push the ring onto her finger, pull her body against mine, and kiss her.

I break our kiss but don't pull away. "We're engaged," I breathe against her lips, the gravity of them only starting to sink in.

She laughs. "I love you so much."

I kiss her again before pulling back enough to admire her. I'm going to spend the rest of my life working my ass off to keep her as happy as she in this moment.

Suddenly, she gasps. "I have to tell Bailey!"

We giggle as I snap a picture of her posing with her ring and she sends it to Bailey. I pull her back into my arms and squeeze her, thinking about all the ways I can show her how much it means to me to call her mine when her phone buzzes.

She answers the call and has to hold the phone out away from her ear when Bailey's high-pitched shriek blares out of the speaker.

"Oh my God!" Bailey yells. "I'm so happy for you! Switch it to a video call, I need to see it!"

Astrid takes a small step away from me and switches to a video call. She holds out her hand in front of her and uses the regular camera to show off her rock, rather than the front-facing camera.

Bailey screams again. "I did not want to see your fiancé's penis!"

I jump to the side. I had completely forgotten that I was still naked from the shower.

"Sorry Bailey!" I say from the dresser where I'm fumbling to find a pair of boxers to throw on. "Astrid found the ring while I was in the shower. In all the excitement, I forgot I wasn't dressed yet."

Astrid laughs and just keeps on showing off her ring.

"It's gorgeous, babe," Bailey says. "Congratulations. You deserve nothing but happiness."

"Thank you," Astrid says to her best friend, tears welling up in her eyes.

"Oh, and congrats on your fiancé's huge dick. Seriously, well done." Bailey laughs.

"I'm hanging up on you now. I'll talk to you later."

Astrid throws the phone down onto the bed as I wrap my arms back around her. I run my nose down the delicate column of her neck and revel in the fact that I can do just that for the rest of my life.

"You're wearing way too many clothes," I murmur into the shell of her ear.

"Well, future *husband*," she says, "feel free to do something about that."

I snicker. "Oh, I plan on it, future *wife*."

Our mouths crash together. I give her a relentless kiss, and in seconds, we're both pulling at her clothing, trying to remove the physical barriers between us. Moments later, I'm hovering over her on the bed, the tip of my cock grazing her slick heat.

"Say it," I say against her mouth. "Say that you're mine."

"I'm yours," she whispers.

I press into her, feeling her tight walls constrict around my cock. She lets out the sexiest gasp when I'm all the way inside.

"Say it again," I murmur as I kiss down her neck as I slowly draw my cock out until only the tip is left inside her sweet pussy.

"I'm yours," she whimpers.

She no sooner has the words out than I slam back into her. I set a punishing pace, nailing her to the mattress with my thrusts, unable to hold back the sheer animal lust I feel knowing she's not going anywhere. She's mine. And I'm going to spend the rest of my life showing her just how much having her means to me in every way possible.

Thank you for reading Cameron and Astrid's story!

Come back this fall for next installment, Reid and Jess's story!

Milton Keynes UK
Ingram Content Group UK Ltd.
UKHW020751190424
441445UK00014B/618